MUST LOVE PETS
Bunny Bonanza

MUST LOVE PETS

Bunny Bonanza

Saadia Faruqi

SCHOLASTIC INC.

Copyright © 2023 by Saadia Faruqi

All rights reserved. Published by Scholastic Inc., *Publishers since 1920*. SCHOLASTIC and associated logos are trademarks and/or registered trademarks of Scholastic Inc.

The publisher does not have any control over and does not assume any responsibility for author or third-party websites or their content.

ISBN 978-1-338-78348-3

10 9 8 7 6 5 4 3 2 1   23 24 25 26 27

Printed in the U.S.A. 40

First printing 2023

Book design by Yaffa Jaskoll

For my first (and only) feathered pet

CHAPTER 1

"Strawberry and kiwi shouldn't go together, but they totally do," I declare.

I'm slouched in a shiny red seat at my favorite café, Tasty, with my favorite people, my besties, London and Olivia. In my hand is the best smoothie known to mankind: Strawberry Kiwi. At Tasty, they're served in tall glasses with thick paper straws.

Very fancy, right?

It's not just the smoothies, though. Everything about the inside of this café is dreamy and pastel colored, like you've stepped through a magical portal or something. I could stay here forever.

"I prefer Berry Berry Wild," London says, wrinkling her nose. She's not a big fan of kiwi.

Olivia slurps noisily through her straw. "I think I agree."

I pretend to glare at her. "Traitor!"

Olivia sticks her smoothie-coated tongue out at me.

"Ew, gross!" I cry. "Amir's rubbing off on you!" Amir is my six-year-old brother and the king of grossness. Olivia adores him, which I kinda get because he's super adorable when he wants to be.

Still, eating with his mouth wide-open is a signature Amir move. Disgusting.

My disgust makes Olivia even bolder. She leans closer and crosses her eyes. "What's gross about me, huh, Imaan? Huh?"

"You're weird," I tell her, trying not to laugh. She knows I don't really mean it, even though we haven't known each other very long. She and her family moved into the neighborhood just a few weeks ago. Now we're not only best friends, but also business partners in a pet-sitting company called Must Love Pets.

Olivia may be awesome, but she's also weird. A good kind of weird.

She sits back, arms across her chest. "Weird because I like berries?"

"Berries are the strangest!" I insist. "Like blueberries, so tart they shouldn't even be a fruit! And raspberries have those tiny hairs on them. What's up with that?"

Olivia's eyes widen. "Kiwis literally have hairy skin!"

I shrug and sip some more smoothie. "But they're delicious."

London throws a wrapper at me. She hates it when people argue in front of her. "Stop, you children!"

Olivia and I grin at each other. "Sorry, Mom!" I say. Unlike Olivia, I've known London forever. Since we were babies, to be exact. I don't even remember our first meeting. We were probably in diapers.

Ew, why did I just think of that? I hate anything poop related, which isn't ideal for someone taking care of animals.

Olivia is slurping her smoothie almost like a challenge. I turn to her and whisper, "You know I'm right. Strawberry Kiwi would win all the awards!"

"Oh yeah?"

"Yeah!"

We stare at each other, fighting our grins. Then we both pick up our glasses and clink them together like we're fancy ladies. "Cheers!" she says.

"Go for the berries—see if I care!" I reply.

"You two should have a competition," London muses. "Take a survey and see how many people like each smoothie. It's called market research."

I put my fist next to my ear, pretending to be on the

phone. "Hey, London, *Shark Tank* called. They said they already have enough actual sharks, thank you very much!"

London glares at me. She's a huge *Shark Tank* fan and probably the only person who watches the show with pen and notepad in hand. Olivia and I dissolve into giggles at London's fierce expression.

"I could be a shark one day," London mutters.

I stop laughing and give her a sideways hug. "Definitely," I assure her. If anyone can grow up to be an amazing entrepreneur one day, it's London. She knows so much about business, it's unreal. Plus, she wears smart suit jackets with the sleeves rolled up like a boss lady.

We start talking about the latest *Shark Tank* episode. We watched it together at London's house two days ago. It was a lot of fun, even though I only understood about 60 percent. London translated the rest of the 40 percent in easy fifth-grade language.

Olivia finishes her smoothie and starts taking

pictures of Tasty on her fancy camera. The red booths. The wood tables. The plate of cookies we're sharing. *Click-click-click.*

"Show me," I say, leaning over her shoulder to look at the LCD display. Olivia is really shy about her photography, but I want her to be proud of it. Her pictures saved us from a total disaster when some naughty kittens we were pet-sitting destroyed our neighbor Mr. Greene's art. Olivia offered to give him a few of her pictures to sell in his Etsy store in exchange for the ones he lost.

Taking care of animals is no joke. Sometimes it gets downright stressful being co-owners of Must Love Pets. Our goal was to convince Mama that I'm responsible enough for a dog, but somehow every new client is Trouble with a capital *T.*

Olivia scrolls through the pictures. "Live-action shots are the best."

"Like the kittens," I say, still thinking of the

mischievous trio. Their names were Missy, Clyde, and Bella, and they were hilarious.

Olivia finds a picture of Amir sitting on the floor. The kittens are all over him like he's a jungle gym. "Amir is just as adorable as the kittens." Olivia giggles.

"Not really," I say, rolling my eyes. Amir is a pain in the behind. But I admit that the picture is cute.

"You should frame this one," London says.

Olivia shrugs. "Maybe."

I already know she's never going to do it. London and I exchange looks. I wag my eyebrows. It's my mission to make Olivia proud and excited about her pictures. I just have to think of the perfect way to do it so she doesn't get embarrassed or mad.

Piece of cake.

"Hello," comes a familiar voice behind us. We turn around, already smiling.

It's Angie, the tall, brown-haired owner of Tasty.

She's wearing a pink-and-white-striped apron with the words QUEEN OF THE KITCHEN on it. "What a lovely camera, new girl," she continues.

New girl—ahem, Olivia—smiles shyly. "Thanks. It was a gift from my dad."

"Do you take good pictures?" Angie asks.

Olivia shrugs. "They're okay."

"They're incredible!" I jump in. "She's a great photographer. Some of her pictures are selling on Etsy."

"Really?" Angie looks very impressed. "Well, all the more reason to ask you kids for help."

"Help with what?" Olivia asks.

Angie places a glossy paper flyer on the table. "'Silverglen Street Party,'" I read. "'Food tastings, music, and more!'"

"That's this Saturday!" Olivia exclaims. "Where will it be?"

"Right here in the parking lot," Angie replies. "I'll

be passing out smoothie samples, plus I have a few food trucks signed up as well. The rest is . . . more difficult."

"The rest?" I ask.

"Kid-friendly entertainment," Angie explains. "I have some giant speakers for music, but I'm not sure what else to organize for the neighborhood kids. I'm too busy and not creative like you girls."

Olivia blushes at being called creative. I wag my eyebrows at London again.

London taps the flyer. "'And more!'" she reads. "That's what you need."

"More what?" I ask.

"That's the million-dollar question, isn't it? That's what I need help with," Angie says very seriously, like we're plotting some super-secret spy mission. "Are you in?"

London, of course, is immediately in. "We'll help you come up with awesome entertainment!" she gushes. "I know lots of people."

"What people?" I ask suspiciously.

"You'll see," London replies with a little smile. "Don't worry, Angie, we'll help."

Angie smiles too, and her shoulders sag a little like she's dropped a huge burden. "Oh, thank you, London!"

London holds up a finger. "In return . . ."

Angie's smile slips. "Yes?"

Olivia and I look at London in alarm. Kids usually don't point fingers at adults and ask for things in return. I kick her under the table, but she moves away. "We don't want payment," I say.

"Not payment," London agrees. "Maybe free smoothies or something?"

Olivia, Angie, and I all stare at her. Wow, *Shark Tank* has really made my best friend a tough negotiator.

Finally, Angie nods. "You girls do this right and you'll get free smoothies for life."

CHAPTER 2

We go back to my house to talk about the street party. "Is your mom working?" Olivia asks a little nervously at the front door. The last time my friends came to my house, Mama threw a temper tantrum and pulled up fence pickets with her bare hands.

She's not usually like that. She'd been upset about our latest pet clients—those pesky kittens—escaping from a hole in the fence and leading us on a merry chase.

To say that Mama is not a fan of Must Love Pets would be an understatement. This is a big problem.

Mama now thinks all animals are evil monsters bent on making her life miserable.

"Don't worry," I say as we head inside. "She's probably in her office at the back of the house. She won't even know we're here."

I'm wrong. Mama is kneeling on the kitchen floor with a sponge. There's an upturned bowl nearby, with something brown and soggy spilled all around. Yuck. One of the chairs is lying on the floor with its legs in the air. "What happened?" I cry.

Mama looks up and sighs. "Your brother insisted on carrying his soup all over the kitchen. Then he tripped and fell into the chair."

"Is he okay?" Olivia asks.

"Just a little cut on his forehead," Mama replies. "Dada Jee took care of it with a Superman bandage."

Dada Jee is my grandfather, and he's supposed to

supervise Amir while Mama works. Unfortunately, Amir is too hyper for Dada Jee.

"Poor baby," Olivia croons.

I roll my eyes. "Poor Dada Jee," I say. "Imagine having to handle that bawling kid!"

"They're fine," Mama says. "They went to get some ice cream and drive around the neighborhood."

I'm glad. Amir loves both ice cream and long rides in our car. If he's got both at the same time, he's in heaven.

London quickly kneels down and takes the sponge from Mama. "We can finish that, Mrs. Bashir."

Mama sighs. "Are you sure? You girls probably have other things to do."

I take her hand and pull her up. "Nothing important," I say. "We'll clean up here so you can get back to work."

Mama stands up and straightens her clothes. "Thank you," she says softly. She starts to leave, then turns back. "Oh, I almost forgot. There was a call on the home phone a little while ago. I'd have picked up, but I was dealing with your brother."

I turn toward the front hallway. You can only see a little glimpse of it from the kitchen, but I imagine the old cordless phone ringing off the hook. "That's our Must Love Pets line."

"Or it could be a telemarketer," Olivia points out. "They call my house all the time, even though we just moved here and got a new number."

I want to howl. What if there was a pet emergency that only we could solve? What if we lost a client because we didn't pick up the phone? Ugh, running a business is really hard. You had to plan for everything. Even little brothers getting hurt and moms not picking the phone up like they're supposed to. "I put a little notepad for messages on the table," I mumble. "And a little pen with a string so it doesn't get lost."

"They'll call again," London says.

"Yup," agrees Olivia. "In the meantime, let's get cleaning!"

It takes us ten minutes to clean up all the mess, straighten the chairs, and wipe down the counters. There are some groceries lying on the counter, so we put them in the pantry. Then London decides to arrange all the spices in alphabetical order. I realize we're all hanging out in the kitchen so we can dash to the phone as soon as it rings.

The phone is silent. It's like that saying, *A watched pot never boils*. Only in our case a watched phone never rings.

Finally, the kitchen is spotless, and there's literally nothing else to do. I drag London and Olivia toward the staircase. "Let's go to my room. If we leave the door open, we'll hear the phone."

"If it rings," Olivia mutters. "Maybe it never will."

I don't reply. She's just being silly. Of course it will ring. It will ring when the universe is ready to send us our next client.

We flop on to the shaggy carpet in my room. London takes out the street party flyer from her jeans pocket and inspects it like it's a clue to a mystery. "'Food tastings, music, and more!'" she reads aloud. "Let's make an ideas list for the *more* part."

I get out a notebook and rip out pages for each of them. "Pens are on the dresser," I tell Olivia.

She's already on her way to my dresser. I know what she's staring at: my arrangement of Happy Meal toys. They're old, from the time when my father was alive and we used to go to McDonald's together for a treat some weekends. "Don't touch my stuff," I warn her but nicely. She already knows how important these silly plastic toys are because we've talked about it before. They're my connection to Baba, and they're precious.

"This one is nice," she says, pointing to a little doll with an angel face and wings.

"I named her Jewel," I say. "Baba said it was a perfect name."

London leans forward from her place on the carpet. "Oh hey, I remember that. I used to have one just like it."

I roll my eyes at her. "That's because we went together that time. Don't you remember?"

She grins slowly. "Oh yeah, we were so happy we got the exact same toy. Your dad was fun!"

I sigh. "Yes, he was."

There's an awkward silence, which I'm very familiar with. People get weird when the topic of Baba comes up, like they're not sure how to deal with it. Olivia grabs the pens from my dresser and hurries back like she's totally regretting ever bringing up the toys in the first place. I squeeze her arm as she sits down next to me. "It's okay to talk about my dad. I don't mind."

"Really?"

I nod. "Yeah, actually, I like it. That's the only way I'll remember him, you know?"

"I remember my grandma from her pictures," she says. "Don't you have pictures of your dad?"

I do, but Mama's packed them up in a box in her closet. "I'll show them to you sometime." We'd have to sneak around behind Mama, though. She'd absolutely not want me digging through her closet.

Oh well, my name's not Imaan Determined Bashir for nothing.

Okay, I just made that up, but it totally suits me, right?

We start writing down our street party ideas suitable for kids. When we're done, we compare notes. I've come up with a clown, a mime, a magician, and a juggler.

"Really, Imaan?" London asks.

"What? They're all cool!"

London reads from her list next. She's got carnival games, a petting zoo, and a photo booth.

"Yes to all these!" Olivia cries.

I'm a tiny bit irritated that London's ideas are so good, but I smile anyway. She's London. Her ideas are always amazing. "We can call everyone we met at the farmers' market last week," she continues. "They'll be happy to get free publicity."

Olivia waves her paper around. "I think there should be an artist making drawings for people."

"Oooh, I like that idea!" I say. "Like caricatures!"

"Do you know anyone who does that?" London asks.

Olivia thinks for a while. "I can ask my dad. He's not bad at drawing."

I raise my eyebrows. I hardly know Olivia's parents, but her dad doesn't look like the artistic type. Then

I think of old Mr. Greene with his frowny face and tattooed arms. You'd never guess that he's an amazing photographer. "Let's do it!" I say.

We're chatting about our plans, laughing at one another's ideas, when I freeze.

RRRING! RRRING!

It's the phone from downstairs. Our Must Love Pets line.

CHAPTER 3

London, Olivia, and I all jump up like we've been bitten.
In an instant, we're rushing downstairs, shouting and
pushing one another. It's not our finest moment, I admit.
My foot slips, and I grab the banister before I tumble.

"Take it easy, Imaan!" London hisses.

"Hurry," I hiss back. There's no way I'm missing
this phone call. It's been several days since our last
animal clients, and I can't wait to see who's next.

"It could be someone selling car insurance," Olivia
squeaks. She's out of breath, but she turns to steady me
with one hand.

"Probably," I reply. "Still, we should check."

London doesn't say anything else because she's smart and knows silent people are faster than those who chatter as they're rushing down the stairs. She reaches the hallway on the fourth ring and grabs the phone. "Must Love Pets. How may I help you?"

Olivia and I reach her, doubled over as we pant. If we ever took part in a marathon, we'd absolutely, positively come in dead last. "Who is it?" I wheeze.

London waves a hand to shush me. "Yes, that's right," she says in the phone. "No job is too small."

I squint. What does that even mean? Too small? Does someone want us to take care of bugs? An ant farm? A roach colony? Ew ew ew, no thanks!

Olivia shakes her head at me, like she knows exactly what I'm thinking. I stick my tongue out at her. "I thought I was in charge of customer service," I whisper.

London glares at me and puts a finger to her lips.

I stick my tongue out at her too. "Customer service picks up the phone, always," I whisper again. Now that I've caught my breath, I'm really feeling the injustice of this entire situation.

Olivia giggles a little. "Maybe run faster next time?" she suggests.

I think back a few seconds to how we'd both teetered on the stairs like toddlers. "OMG!" I whisper. "That was—"

"HUSH!" London's glare is even fiercer now.

I feel bad for distracting her. *Sorry,* I mouth.

She takes up the notebook and pen that are next to the phone and starts scribbling. Olivia and I lean over her shoulder to see.

Sonya Q.

Rabbit

1 week

Trained

I practically jump in excitement. I love rabbits! I've seen a few scampering about in the neighborhood park, and they look so cuddly. It's literally been a lifelong dream to hold a soft rabbit in my arms and just . . . pet it.

Okay, yeah, that sounds a bit creepy. But spending a whole week with a cutie-pie bunny rabbit sounds like the absolute best.

London's still talking to Sonya Q. "Thank you for trusting us with your pet," she says in her most soothing voice. "We will take care of him like family." I give her a thumbs-up because she is making the customer service department very proud right now.

London takes down more information, like a phone number and email address—we send very official emails with rates and instructions, just like a real company. Then she puts the phone down and grins. "Soooo . . ."

"A rabbit! Yay!" Olivia says, grinning back.

"We're gonna have so much fun!" I agree, totally hyped. "What's his name?

London spreads her arms wide in a *ta-da* movement. "His name is . . . wait for it . . . Doc."

I don't really understand the silence that follows. "As in *doctor*?" I ask slowly. "That doesn't make sense."

London puts her arms down. "Seriously, Imaan?"

I stare at her. "What?" I know I'm missing something, but I can't tell what it is. Ugh, I hate being clueless.

London isn't going to just tell me, of course. She rolls her eyes. "As in *What's up, Doc?*" Only she says it in a weird, nasally voice. Then she pretends to chew on something loudly.

What on earth is wrong with her? "Nothing's up, Doc," I reply with gritted teeth.

Olivia bursts out laughing. "That was a great impression, London!" She turns to me. "Haven't you ever watched Bugs Bunny cartoons, Imaan?"

Now both my friends are looking at me like I'm an alien from outer space. "Bugs Bunny? Never heard of it. Maybe Amir will know?" I doubt it, though, because all Amir watches are superhero cartoons. His current favorite is Superman.

Olivia takes pity on me and stops laughing. She pats my arm. "It's an old cartoon about a really clever rabbit called Bugs Bunny."

"Yeah, he totally outsmarts all the other characters who are out to get him!" London adds. "A real trickster, that one!"

"Okayyyy . . ." Honestly, I'm not getting what the big deal is. Or how this Bugs Bunny character is related to a doctor.

Olivia continues: "You have to watch the cartoons— they're so funny! Bugs Bunny keeps evading all these traps, and then he sneaks up to his enemies and says, 'Eh, what's up, Doc?' like nothing happened. All the time he's chewing on this carrot like it's a normal afternoon. Drives the enemies bonkers!"

They both start laughing again. My lips twitch too. They're right—Bugs Bunny sounds hilarious, although nothing like the soft, fuzzy rabbit of my dreams. "I'll check out the cartoon," I say.

Olivia claps her hands. "Ooh, maybe we can watch some episodes together at our next sleepover!"

I raise my eyebrow at her. Mama has never let me have sleepovers until this summer, when the three of us had our first movie night. I don't want to push my luck again so soon. "We'll see. You wanna talk about our actual client now?"

So here are the details of our newest client: Sonya Q. is an animal trainer who makes online videos for new pet owners. Her office building had a small fire—yikes!—and she's putting her animals in a safe place until she can find a new space. We go back upstairs to my room and search for Sonya. Her full name is Sonya the Animal Trainer Queen. It's obviously not her real name, but it sounds super cool so I'm going to pretend that's what it says on her birth certificate. Her website has a bunch of videos, mostly of rabbits, dogs, and cats. But there's also one with a big snake, and another with a bunch of penguins at a zoo.

"Wow, she's awesome!" Olivia sighs.

I click play on the latest video. Sonya is training a medium-sized black-and-white rabbit how to jump through a hoop. "Wow, I didn't realize rabbits could do tricks," I mutter, a little mad at myself for not knowing this amazing fact.

"Yeah, they have bunny-jumping competitions and everything," Olivia replies. "I saw it on TV once."

"My mind is officially blown!" I watch the video

to the end and get started on another. It's a more basic one, about caring for a pet rabbit, grooming it, even teaching it to poop in a litter box—I fast-forward through that part. Sonya is holding the black-and-white rabbit in her arms again. His ears are long and floppy, and his nose twitches very fast.

"Do you think that's Doc?" I ask. He looks so cute!

London shrugs. "I'm not sure," she says. "Maybe?"

"She has a bunch of animals, right?" Olivia asks. "Are we keeping all of them?"

I freeze. Don't get me wrong, I love animals. But I don't think we can take care of a whole group of them together. Mama would absolutely freak out.

"No, of course not," London replies. "She's found temporary homes for all of them except Doc. She says it's because he needs a place with kids. He's not happy with only adults."

"Same here," I joke. "Adults are no fun to be around."

"Your Dada Jee is," London points out.

I beam at her because that's the perfect response. Anyone who likes my Dada Jee as much as I do is a perfect human being.

"Speaking of your grandfather, where is he?" Olivia asks.

The front door slams open, and we hear a loud, cranky yell. "Why are there shoes lying in the hall? Do you girls want me to fall down and break my hip?"

CHAPTER 4

We find Dada Jee in the kitchen, washing his hands in the sink. "Salaam, Dada Jee," I say.

He grunts at us. Typical.

"Look, Imaan, ice cream!" Amir calls. He's at the kitchen table, finishing up his ice-cream cone. Or rather, smearing it all over his face. Ugh.

I grab a paper towel from the counter and wipe the smears from his cheeks and nose. "Looks delicious," I say, trying not to laugh.

"Where's my share?" Olivia asks, hands on hips.

He holds out his half-eaten, very gross cone. "You can have this. I don't want any more."

"Ew!" London says, shuddering.

I gently push the cone back toward his mouth. "No, she's good."

Olivia grins at Amir. "We had smoothies at Tasty anyway."

"This is better than Tasty," Amir boasts.

"Careful what you say, buddy," I warn him. "Tasty is the best in the entire world, right, Dada Jee?"

Dada Jee sits down on a chair with a sigh. "I suppose," he says gruffly. "Their lemon soufflé is legendary."

"Sure!" I give him a knowing look. Dada Jee is a lemon expert. He grows his own lemons in our backyard and sometimes sells them to places like Tasty. Last week, he even sold several buckets of lemons in a farmers' market.

Is it weird that he treats his lemons like they're babies? Maybe.

Is it weird that he talks to the trees as he prunes them? Definitely.

Dada Jee isn't your typical grandfather. He lived most of his life in a village in Pakistan. He only came to the U.S. a few years ago when Baba died, to help Mama take care of us. Since then, he's learned English, grown a million lemons, and basically managed Amir every single day. Weird or not, the man deserves an award.

I lean over and hug him. "Tasty's lemon soufflé is very good," I assure him.

He scowls. "What's wrong with you, girl?"

I lean back with a grin. "Nothing."

"Did Angie tell you she's having a street party?" London asks. "You should set up a lemonade stall there, Dada Jee."

"London, please!" I beg. Dada Jee may be awesome,

but that doesn't mean everyone's a fan of his lemon obsession. Mama, for example. She almost freaked out when Dada Jee took his lemons to the farmers' market. She thinks his lemons distract him from our family.

Mama's wrong, of course, but who's brave enough to tell her that?

"Wait a minute," Dada Jee says, looking very interested. "A party on a street? What for?"

London explains what a street party is. He listens carefully, nodding. "Americans and their strange ways," he says slowly. "And Angie wants me to sell my lemonade there?"

"Not sell," Olivia says. "It's a party, so you'd be giving out samples. That way, people will get to know how good your lemonade is."

"It's delicious," London adds, like she hasn't told him that a thousand times before.

I roll my eyes at her.

"What? It's true," she says, shrugging.

I open my mouth to reply, but just then there's a crash from the living room. "Amir!" I gasp. That sneaky kid has disappeared out of the kitchen from right under our noses and is now probably running around the house with ice-cream hands.

Dada Jee shakes his head. "It's fine, I'll get him!" He stands up with the help of his cane, then heads toward the living room. In the doorway he turns and points his cane at us. "Sign me up for that party on the street!"

London pumps her fist in the air. "YES!"

London is on a roll. She's made up an entertainment list for Angie's street party, only she's being businesslike and calling it "the talent." I imagine rock stars and comedians. She goes over her list and checks it off like the competent person she is. She's got a clipboard and everything!

"Okay, so we have the smoothie and food samples from Tasty, plus the lemonade samples from your granddad," she says, tapping her pen on the clipboard. "Now for the fun part."

"What fun part?" I ask.

We're standing in the cul-de-sac outside our houses, London's and mine on one side, and Olivia's on the other. It's early evening, and we're meeting for some fresh air. "Booking the talent!" London smiles very big, like she's a game show host talking about the big prize.

"Right here on the street?" I ask, my eyes wide. "There's no talent here. Most people I know are actually the opposite of talented."

"Talent doesn't have to be something incredible," London says patiently.

I'm impressed, obviously, but also confused. "What is even happening right now?" I ask. "Angie asked us to figure out some kid-friendly entertainment. That's all."

"Those were her exact words," Olivia agrees.

London clutches her clipboard to her chest. "So? That's what I'm doing."

"No, no." I point to her clipboard like it's exhibit A in a courtroom drama. "You're finding talent. That's . . . too much. I was thinking a face-painting booth or something. Remember our list?"

London shakes her head and starts walking. "That's basic. We need next-level. We're professionals."

I start to say that wasn't the assignment Angie gave us, but then I remember that London has literally never done only the basic assignments in school. She always does the extra credit too. That's just how she is. I exchange looks with Olivia and follow London.

"We'll ask around. Everyone here must have some hobby or skill they can share."

My mouth drops open. "You're not serious. We can't go knocking on doors and asking about people's hobbies!"

"Why not?"

I sputter. "Why not, London? It's . . . inappropriate. Remember how much we all hate those door-to-door salespeople? The ones who sell magazine subscriptions or dish antennas or other random stuff nobody wants? Also, our moms will be mad."

London waves a hand like I'm making a big deal about nothing. "It's not like I'm really knocking on doors, Imaan." She turns to Olivia. "Is your dad home yet? We could ask him about the caricatures."

Olivia nods to the truck in her driveway. "Seems like it. Wanna come inside?"

I glance back at my house. It's almost dinnertime, and I need to help Mama in the kitchen.

"We're having pizza," Olivia says in a singsong voice.

I look at London. She's still grinning, and tapping her clipboard on her leg like she's got some evil plan up her sleeve. "Maybe just for a little while," I reply.

Olivia's dad is in the living room watching football on TV. "How are you girls?" he asks in a booming voice.

Olivia tells him about the street party and how we're looking for entertainment.

"*Talent*," London inserts. "That's the official word for it."

He looks puzzled. "Like an act?"

"Kind of, only it's not a circus!" Olivia tries laughing, but he's frowning now, so she stops.

"What do you need from me?" he asks. It's obvious he wants to go back to his football game.

Olivia swallows like she's suddenly nervous. I jump in. "Mr. Gordon, could you draw people? Like caricatures?"

"Me? Draw?"

"You don't have to be good," I assure him. "It's just for fun. We're not expecting great art or anything."

"Well, that's a relief."

Olivia clasps her hands together. "Please, Dad?" she whispers. "It'll just be for a few hours and it will be so much help to Angie!"

"I don't even know this Angie person."

"But you know us," London says. "And we're asking you to help us."

He looks at all three of us. I think he's going to say no, but he shakes his head and asks, "When is this party? I work some weekends, you know."

I say, "This Saturday at ten."

"Can you do it?" Olivia asks anxiously.

He rubs a hand on his chin. "I'm not sure. I'll have to check my schedule. Sometimes the boss wants me to come in on Saturdays. He'll let me know tomorrow."

Mr. Gordon is the assistant manager at a home improvement store. Olivia says he has to work more than usual because he's the newbie. Everyone gives him extra work and he can't say no.

I feel bad for him. I give him my best smile and say, "Perfection!"

Olivia giggles. London rolls her eyes at me. "What?" I say. "He's going to let us know tomorrow. That's basically a promise, right?"

Mr. Gordon shakes his head again like he thinks the three of us are funny. "I'll try my best," he says firmly, and goes back to the football game.

"That's good enough for us," London says.

"Perfection!" Olivia says, giggling again. She drags us toward the kitchen. "Pizza time!"

CHAPTER 5

Sonya arrives the next morning. I recognize her face when I open the door, but I'm still shocked because She. Is. Tall. Her height wasn't obvious from the videos we watched. "Hello," she says in a brisk voice. "We talked on the phone about my rabbit?"

I remind myself about customer service and smile. "Yes, that's right. I'm Imaan from Must Love Pets."

She doesn't smile back. "I spoke with someone called London."

My smile slips a little. "She'll be here soon. She lives right next door."

"Okay, I'll wait."

"Er, you don't need to wait. I can help you. We're partners, the three of us."

She frowns. "There are three of you?"

"Yes!" I say quickly. "Me, London, and our third friend, Olivia."

Sonya looks like she's digesting this information. "Is this Olivia also your next-door neighbor?"

I nod and point across the street. "We all live close by, plus we're best friends. And business partners!" I smile again, bigger this time. That's what customer service is all about, isn't it? Showing happiness while taking care of clients?

"Oh Lord," Sonya mutters. "So how long will your business partners be? I need to get going!"

I keep smiling although my jaw is starting to hurt now. "That's what I was trying to tell you. No need to wait. You can just hand over your pet to me and feel comfortable that we'll take good care of it."

"How can I feel comfortable if I've only met one person in a three-person business?"

I'm not sure how to answer her. She's technically right. I'd want to meet everyone who was taking care of my pet too. Thankfully, I see movement on our driveway. "There they are!" I say, sighing in relief.

London walks smartly toward us. She's dressed perfectly in light-blue jeans and her favorite black suit jacket. Olivia is right behind her, also wearing jeans and a white blouse with fluffy sleeves. I feel totally underdressed in my yoga pants and faded T-shirt.

"Welcome to Must Love Pets!" London cries as she jogs up the porch steps. "I'm so sorry we're late!"

"Hmph!" Sonya replies, but she's lost her frown. "No problem."

I wave my hand at my friends. "That's London," I say. "And behind her is Olivia."

Sonya looks at the three of us with narrowed eyes like she's trying to read our minds. "I hope you girls know what you're doing."

I'm immediately annoyed. She'd asked questions yesterday during her call, and later I'd emailed her all sorts of information, including testimonials from our previous clients. What else did this lady need?

London says, "We definitely know what we're doing, ma'am. We've taken care of lots of pets before."

"Yup," Olivia adds cheerfully. "Kittens and goats and dogs and squirrels . . ."

"Oh my!" Sonya says.

This is something out of *The Wizard of Oz*, right? I've watched that movie so many times with Mama and Dada Jee that I recognize the lyrics right away. *Lions and tigers and bears, oh my!* Is Sonya teasing Olivia? I doubt it because Sonya's face is completely blank. Not a hint of a smile. She's as tall and straight and unbending as a tree, holding a big animal carrier in her hand.

Then I notice a glint in her eye. I relax a little. Maybe Sonya is the kind of person who has a really weird sense of humor. "Funny," I say.

She just raises her eyebrows at me, like she has no idea what I'm talking about.

"So, is that Doc?" Olivia asks, pointing to the carrier in her hand.

Sonya sighs, like she's finally given up resisting our charms. "Yes, this is Doc. Can I come inside so I can show you everything he'll need?"

I step aside and open the front door wide. "Welcome to Must Love Pets," I say very loudly, my smile back on my face.

"Oh Lord," she mutters again as she passes me.

*   *   *

Sonya may not trust our experience in pet sitting, but we've actually learned a lot in the last few weeks. Here are some of my most important lessons:

1. A pet must have its own space away from the Bashir family.

2. A pet must have some sort of cage or enclosure so it doesn't run away.

3. Pet sitters must prepare for a pet's arrival ahead of time.

How did we learn all these lessons? The hard way, of course. When we'd taken care of our neighbor's dog, he'd sat on Dada Jee's beloved chair, making my poor grandfather furious. Then we'd taken care of three hyperactive kittens who'd climbed curtains and stepped into butter on the kitchen table and generally created mayhem. That made Mama furious.

All this because we weren't prepared.

So last night, London, Olivia, and I had prepped like

bosses. We'd cleared out a small room off the hallway that was originally a dining room but is now used for storage. Amir's old playpen from the garage has been cleaned and lined with blankets. A small plastic bowl sits in the corner, ready for food or water. There's a lot of open space around the playpen for animals to run around if they want.

Olivia's even propped a small chalkboard on the windowsill, with the words *Welcome to Must Love Pets* and then a blank space. Now she walks over to it and writes *DOC* in big white chalk, then a smiley face.

I grin because I absolutely love this little room. I want to say, *Ta-da!* but I stop myself. Will Sonya think this is good enough? She's probably seen really fancy setups by actual pet-sitting corporations.

I have no clue what she's thinking, though. She takes her time, staring at every single thing in the room silently. The storage boxes and household odds and ends have been pushed to the far corners of the room, but she can definitely see them. I know I should have removed them, but Mama wouldn't have wanted that.

In fact, Mama doesn't know yet that we'd transformed this room from storage to pet-sitting area. I try not to think of what she'll say when she sees it.

I swallow. "Well?" I ask.

Sonya kneels on the floor and puts Doc's carrier down gently. "It's good," she replies. "Really good."

London, Olivia, and I break out into relieved grins. "Phew!" Olivia says. "Glad you like it. Isn't the chalkboard a nice touch?"

Sonya's eye has got that glint again. I'm sure she's amused, but her face doesn't show it. "Want to see Doc?" she asks.

We all nod like bobblehead dolls.

She unzips the carrier and reaches in with both hands. I lean forward to look, but I can't see anything. I bite my lip before I tell Sonya to hurry up. Somehow, I don't think she's going to like that.

Finally, her hands come back out. She's holding a soft black-and-white bunny rabbit with floppy ears and a quivering pink nose, just like the one in the videos I watched. "OMG!" I squeal.

Beside me, London and Olivia are literally vibrating with excitement. "He's adorable!" Olivia breathes.

Sonya's face finally splits into a tiny smile. "Girls, meet Doc. He's a Holland Lop, and he's five years old."

"Can we pet him?" I ask breathlessly, my hand hovering over Doc's head.

"Just a finger over his head, gently."

I do exactly what Sonya says, and my finger sinks into the softness of Doc's fur. "Hello, baby," I whisper.

Doc looks at me and his whole body seems to quiver. I think he's saying hello, but I can't be sure.

I wish I spoke bunny. That would be so cool.

London is next with a finger on Doc's head, and then Olivia gets a turn. They're both grinning ear to ear. "Soft, right?" I ask them.

Olivia nods and sighs, like she doesn't have words for the level of softness of Doc's head.

Sonya straightens up and puts Doc into the playpen. "He needs time to get used to people, so don't touch him too much," she says. "I'll bring in his food and litter box and help you set everything up."

Olivia picks up a clipboard that's been lying on the windowsill next to her chalkboard. "What about his routine?" she asks. "Does he need exercise? How many times do we feed him?"

"Great questions!" Sonya looks impressed. Finally.

She opens her mouth to answer, but just then a hurricane whooshes into the room.

AKA my pesky brother, Amir.

CHAPTER 6

"Imaan, do you have a new animal? Let me see! LET ME SEE!"

Amir screeches to a halt right next to me. For a second his little body sways as if it's not sure it's actually going to stop moving. I grip his hand. "Hush, Amir," I whisper.

"I wanna see the animal," he repeats. Loudly.

I cringe. How am I supposed to bring my best customer service if my own brother is going to be so rowdy and extra? "You will," I say. "Can you say hi to our client, Ms. Sonya, first?"

Amir looks up shyly at Sonya. "Hi," he whispers. I thank my lucky stars that he gets shy around strangers.

"Hello, young man," Sonya replies. "Are you also part of Must Love Pets?"

He opens his eyes wide, like this has never occurred to him before. "I helped make the flyers," he offers.

"And he plays with the animals to keep them company," London adds.

This is very true. Amir can be a big help if he calms down and follows directions.

I squeeze his hand, but he lets go and turns toward the playpen. "Is it another kitty?" He spies Doc sniffing around the edges of the enclosure, and jumps with excitement. "A bunny rabbit!"

I reach over and grab the back of Amir's shirt because he's in danger of falling into the playpen in his hurry to get to Doc. "Easy, Amir, we don't want to scare him. Everything is new here. He needs time to adjust."

"Oh." Amir looks disappointed. "I really wanted to hold him."

I can't even look at Amir's face right now, all adorable with a trembling lip and big eyes. Ugh, he knows exactly how to get his own way!

Sonya seems immune, though. She points a finger at Amir. "Be good, and stay quiet. Doc will probably be your best friend before long."

"Really?"

"Really. He gets scared easily, but if you stay with him for a while, he'll get used to you."

Amir stands very still. "I can do that. Right, Imaan?"

I highly doubt he can stay quiet and unmoving for longer than five seconds, but I nod anyway. "You can do anything you put your mind to, buddy."

We stand side by side, watching Doc. My fingers itch to stroke his head again, but there's no way I'm doing that in front of Amir. After a while, Sonya leaves to get the rest of the things from her car. Olivia and London follow to help her.

No surprise, Amir loses all his shyness as soon as we're alone. "I want to touch him. Why can't I touch him?" he whines.

I let out a huge sigh. "Okay, fine, you can touch him for just a second."

"Yay!"

I lean over the pen and try grabbing Doc. He quickly hops away.

I walk a few steps in his direction and try again. Nope, he's quicker than me again.

"Hurry, Imaan!" Amir's whine is louder now.

"I'm trying!"

"What's the problem?" he demands. "Just pick him up."

I grit my teeth. It's not as easy as it sounds. This rabbit doesn't want to be caught.

Amir stomps his foot and opens his mouth for a full-on scream. I absolutely don't want Mama or Dada Jee to hear him, so I make a big grab for Doc and end up pushing against the playpen's soft walls.

And then I'm falling.

"Oof!" I teeter for a second, then fall right inside the pen. One foot tangles in a blanket. One arm brushes against soft rabbit fur.

Then Doc hops away to the farthest end of the playpen.

"Are you okay, Imaan?" Amir asks, sounding tearful.

I blink. "Yeah . . ."

"OMG, what happened?"

Great, Sonya and the girls are back. They're staring at me with their mouths open, like they've never seen someone on her butt before. "Imaan fell in," Amir explains unnecessarily.

"What were you doing?" London gasps.

I grimace. I know how unprofessional this looks, me sprawled all over the playpen, our rabbit client shivering in the corner as far away as he can possibly get from me. Amir standing nearby looking suspiciously innocent, like none of this is his doing.

Ugh. This is a disaster.

"I was just . . ." I stop because I don't know what to say.

"She was trying to catch the bunny for me." Again, Amir is being extremely unhelpful right now.

I glare at him, but since I'm all the way on the floor, I don't think he notices. "I wasn't . . . he's the one who . . ."

Sonya mutters under her breath and steps into the playpen with me, her hand extended. "Come on, get up, young lady."

I take her hand and she pulls me up. I watch as she goes over to Doc and picks him up gently. "You never make sudden movements near rabbits," she tells us. "They're prey animals so they instinctively run away from danger."

"I'm not dangerous," Amir says indignantly.

I'm starting to doubt this, but I keep quiet. No need to hurt his feelings.

Sonya holds Doc out in her arms toward Amir. "Here, you can touch him on the head with a finger. Gently, okay?"

Amir nods and does as he's told. His tongue is sticking out between his lips, like he's working on a very difficult math problem. "Why can't I hold him?" he asks, the whine back in his voice.

I jump out of the playpen. "He's a client, Amir. You have to respect his owner's wishes."

Amir looks at Sonya like she's a dragon. "You shouldn't be selfish," he tells her. "I always share my toys with anyone who asks."

OMG. I cringe again. Apparently, Amir's shyness is all gone. Beside me, Olivia covers her mouth with her hands, eyes wide with shock. London just shakes her head.

I'm expecting Sonya to march right outside with her rabbit. I wouldn't even blame her if she wanted to get away from Must Love Pets forever. But Sonya just grins—her first grin since I've met her. "I'm not being selfish, young man," she says. "Doc is scared right now because he's never seen you before. You can try again later."

Amir thinks about this with squinted eyes. "Okay," he finally says. "I'm hungry." He waves to us, then runs out of the room, shouting for Dada Jee to give him a snack.

Well. That was rude. I turn to Sonya. "I'm sorry . . ."

She puts Doc down. "No need to apologize. I've got nieces and nephews. I understand." She jumps out of the playpen. "Now, let me show you all Doc's things . . ."

We gather around her and gawk at the items she's brought from her car. They're seriously impressive. There are toys like twine balls and fake fruit. There's a cute little brush for Doc's fur, a bag of food pellets, and a big bag of hay.

"Rabbits love hay, and they eat a lot of it," Sonya tells us. "You can give him a couple of baby carrots or a bunch of cilantro as a treat, but not more than once a day."

Perfect. I love baby carrots too.

Then Sonya brings out a black bag and starts taking things out of it. There's a blue fabric tunnel like the ones babies crawl through at playtime, a few hoops, and things that look like toys. Are we going to be taking care of a baby too? I am *so* not ready for this.

I open my mouth to protest, but London beats me to it. "Er, what's all this?"

Sonya grins again. "These are for Doc."

"But they're baby toys."

Sonya looks at us like we've lost it. "They're an obstacle course. I've been training Doc, but he's still new at it. He can't stop for a week because otherwise he'll forget everything he's learned so far."

"Soooo . . . ?" I ask slowly.

"So, you girls have to make sure he remembers."

CHAPTER 7

Wait, what? We have to train a rabbit?

This pet-sitting job just got way more interesting!

Sonya is totally enjoying the looks on our faces. I feel like my mouth is frozen in a big O, and I'm pretty sure I haven't blinked for a while. "We're not trainers . . ." I begin.

London nudges me with her elbow. "We're happy to help, but we'll need to charge you more than our usual fee."

"Ah yes, that's what I was going to say," I finish weakly. I can't believe London's actually asking for more money. Where does she get such bold ideas from?

Shark Tank, obviously. But still.

Sonya chuckles quietly. "Agreed."

"Really?" Olivia squeaks.

"Yes, I'll pay you twice your normal rate if you continue Doc's training routine. It's really easy, and you girls will have fun."

London nods like she's satisfied.

I'm still uneasy, though. "How will we know what to do?"

Sonya kneels on the floor and starts putting the obstacle course together. "Don't worry, I'll teach you."

Right now? This is unreal.

Also, it's pretty cool. We're getting a chance to learn from an actual animal trainer! I remember the videos on her website. Basically, she's a true professional. A thrill runs through me as I watch her set everything up quickly.

It's a little like a magic trick. Each individual part

of the course is small and ordinary looking. A short plastic slide. A fence. Several colorful hoops. And of course the fabric tunnel. Together these small parts make up a pretty awesome obstacle course.

Olivia grabs my hand and squeezes. She's grinning madly. "Can you believe this?" she whispers.

I cannot.

"Doc's going to go through this whole thing?" I ask doubtfully.

"Rabbits are very intelligent, you know," London tells me. "People don't give them enough credit."

"Yes, but is Doc able to do all this?"

Sonya straightens up and goes to fetch Doc. "I guess we'll find out, won't we?" She stands a few paces away from Doc and snaps her fingers. "Come, Doc," she says.

Doc hops right up to her and sniffs her fingers.

She raises her hand until it's up to her waist. "Come, Doc," she repeats.

Doc stands on his hind legs, front paws tucked at his chest.

"Whoa!" I whisper. "He's like . . . a dog."

Sonya wrinkles her nose. "Better. Dogs like to slobber. Rabbits don't." She puts her hand down and turns back to us. Doc gets down to the floor and follows, his nose twitching. They reach the edge of the obstacle course. "Ready for your lesson?" Sonya asks.

"YES!" the three of us say together.

Sonya's right, it's pretty simple. She picks up a bag of treats and takes a few in the palm of her hand. Then she points to the first step of the course, which is the fence. "Let's go, Doc!" she says, holding a treat up on the other side of the fence.

Doc runs up to the fence, then jumps clear over it. "Hooray!" I say, clapping.

"Shh!" London says. "Don't distract him!"

"Sorry."

Doc continues on the course, following Sonya's hand. After each obstacle, she gives him a treat. He nibbles it quickly and heads on to the next part of the course. "OMG, he's so smart!" I whisper to London and Olivia when Doc goes up and down the slide better than any toddler I've ever seen.

London nods. "Yup."

Olivia doesn't say anything. She's got her camera up to her eye, and she's snapping pictures of Doc in motion. *Click–click–click.*

I see a movement from the corner of my eye. Dada Jee and Amir are standing by the doorway. I hope Amir doesn't barge in, like he always does, and make Doc freak out again. Then I notice that Dada Jee is holding his hand in a tight grip.

I give them both a little smile and turn back to watch the brilliant Doc.

He's a super-soft machine! Up, down, over, under,

squeezing through, jumping—he does everything with style. Plus, the signature nose twitch.

Finally, he reaches the end of the course. I clap again, not caring if I'm loud. This bunny rabbit deserves some applause!

Sonya scoops up Doc in her arms and rubs his head over and over. "Good job, baby. Good job!"

"That was amazing!" Amir gushes from his corner. He's now pulling against Dada Jee's hand like he can't wait to get loose. "He's like *American Ninja Bunny Warrior*."

I let out a surprised laugh. "That's true!" Sometimes we watch that show together. Amir loves to hurl himself around the living room, jumping from couch to couch, crawling on the floor, shouting, "Look at me, Imaan!"

"I wanna go next," Amir says, pulling at Dada Jee's hand again.

Dada Jee grunts. "On that obstacle course? You're too big for that, child!"

Sonya looks up at the sound of Dada Jee's voice. "Hello," she says. "Are you also part of Must Love Pets?"

Dada Jee's grunt is even louder this time. "No way. This business is the girls' brainchild. I just get dragged into it whenever there's a disaster."

"Dada Jee!" I whisper furiously. "No talk of disasters!"

Sonya shakes her head. "Well, my building just caught fire and I spent all night hauling a dozen animals out of danger, so I'm not immune to disaster either."

I relax a little. "Sorry about that," I say. "It must have been scary."

"A fire?" Amir asks, fascinated. "Was it huge?"

"Thankfully, no," Sonya replies. "It was a small electrical fire. Nothing too bad. But the animals got upset, and now the landlord has to send people in to fix things."

"Don't worry, we'll take good care of Doc," I say.

"Yes," Amir says. "We're the bestest."

"I think you are," Sonya replies solemnly.

Doc wriggles in Sonya's arms, like he's bored with this entire conversation.

"Should I give him another treat?" London asks, reaching for the bag.

"Just one," Sonya agrees. "You don't want to run out. You have to do this course with him every day."

"No problem," Olivia says, putting down her camera. "I took pictures of the course so we'll know exactly how to set it up next time."

Sonya gives Doc's head one last rub and puts him back into the playpen. He quickly hops to his carrier and disappears inside. "Since you don't have a hutch, the carrier will have to do."

"Sorry . . ." I begin.

"Don't worry about it. He's used to the carrier, so it may actually be more comforting for him."

"Aw, the little guy will miss home," Olivia said, sniffing a little. "How can we make him happy here?"

Sonya grins. "It's very simple. He loves kids, so as long as you don't get too excited around him, you can spend as much time as you want with him."

Amir jumps at this. "Yayy! I want to be his best friend!"

Sonya walks over to him and bends down until they're at eye level. "Will you promise not to scare him?"

Amir quiets down. He nods, his eyes big. "Promise," he whispers.

"That means no running around, or shouting. You have to sit quietly and wait for him to come to you."

Amir's nod is quicker this time. "Yes, I'll do that. Promise!"

Sonya ruffles his hair and stands up straight. "Good. I know you can do it, buddy."

"Don't worry, Sonya," London says. "We'll take excellent care of Doc."

"I'm sure you will." She takes out a card from her pocket and hands it to London. "Call me if anything comes up. I don't mind answering questions."

We all walk Sonya to the front door. When she's gone, Amir tugs at my hand. "No time to waste," he says. "Let's go back and play with Doc."

I groan. "Don't you ever get tired?"

He's already running toward our Pet Room, arms out like an airplane. "Nope!"

CHAPTER 8

"What do you think?" Olivia asks, holding up a piece of white card stock.

I squint. It's supposed to be an invite to the Tasty street party, but it looks more like a wedding invitation. Square, with a flowery border. BORING!

I don't say that, though. "Too formal," I reply instead.

Olivia's mouth falls open. "What are you talking about? It's perfect!"

I roll my eyes. "Only if you're inviting people to a fancy adult party or something."

She sighs and drops it back on her bed. "Ugh, you're right. We need more color."

"Maybe use green card stock instead?" I suggest. "Or, I know! Orange."

"I hate orange."

Now it's my turn for the open mouth. Who doesn't like orange? "It screams fun," I insist.

"It screams horror," Olivia says. "Like Halloween."

"Exactly. Halloween is the most fun."

She throws a marker at me. I catch it and throw it right back. Then we grin at each other.

We're in the Pet Room in my house, sitting cross-legged on the floor. Doc's in the playpen, sleeping on top of a pile of hay in the far corner. He was pretty active in the morning, hopping around, investigating things, playing with his toys. Now, just after noon, he's eaten a bunch of food—more hay!—and gone to sleep. I want to just hang out here, watching his cute little bunny ears twitching as he dreams.

Only I can't because we're supposed to be party planning. It's Tuesday already, which means only four more days until the Big Event. Olivia and I are in charge of what London calls *marketing materials*. In everyday language, this means posters and stuff.

It's not going great, though. We can't even decide on colors.

London is right next to us, lying on her stomach with papers in front of her. "Stop bickering, you two," she says without looking up. "You got the easy job."

This is true. Making posters is way easier than coming up with entertainment for a party. "It's your own fault, London," I say. "You told Angie you'd take care of this."

She looks up, a frown on her face. "I *will* take care of it."

She's so determined. Classic London. But behind the frown is a look of worry. "What do you have so far?" I ask, peering at the scribbles on London's papers.

"Not much so far," she admits. "I called Tamara from the farmers' market and she said she'd bring some animals."

"That's a great idea!" Olivia exclaims.

I smile. Tamara's family has a farm close by, and their goats make a great petting zoo at the local farmers' market each week. "I hope she brings Marmalade," I say. "I miss that old goat."

Marmalade is a Must Love Pets client. He's totally awesome, even though he eats paper for lunch and poops on people's front yards.

By people I mean me. Yes, totally gross.

"What else?" Olivia asks London.

"Hopefully your dad will say yes to our caricature idea," London says. "Oh, and my dad called his friend

Mack who's a firefighter. They're going to bring the truck to show kids."

"Wow, that sounds incredible!"

I say, "Amir is going to be in heaven, with goats and fire trucks and delicious food!"

"Let's face it," Olivia replies. "Me too."

We all laugh at that.

Then London gets all serious. "It's a good start, but we need lots more."

"It's only a small street party, London," I tell her. "You can't go overboard."

London acts like I've said something rude. "I never go overboard."

Olivia and I just stare at her. "Seriously?" I ask. "You're basically Miss Overboard Harrison."

"Good one, Imaan!" Olivia says, holding up her palm for a high five.

I slap her palm with mine. "Thank you." Then I

turn to London. "We're teasing, you know."

"I know."

"But Angie didn't ask you to do all this. She just wanted a little kid-friendly entertainment. What we have is more than enough."

"Totally," Olivia agrees.

London ignores us. "Music!" she says suddenly. "That's the thing that's missing. Know any good bands?"

"Seriously?" I ask again. I realize I'm repeating myself, but I can't help it. Where on earth does she think we'll get a band from?

London gives me a patient look. "Yes, Imaan. We need music. There can be no party without music."

It's not that I disagree. Music and partying definitely go together. It's just that I don't think this is a miracle we can pull off:

A. Find a band in less than a week.

B. Make sure they're actually good.

C. Ask them to perform for free.

Impossible. Right?

Right.

I look at Olivia to back me up.

News flash: Olivia is not backing me up. She's chewing on her lip, deep in thought. "Olivia?" I ask. "Tell London to forget about a band. We can just hook a phone to the speakers and play the latest hits."

"Maybe not . . ." Olivia says slowly.

"YES!" London pumps a fist.

"What?" I can't believe Olivia is encouraging London's overboard-ness. She doesn't know London as well as I do. Encouraging her is the worst thing you can do.

"What if I told you I know someone in a band?" Olivia says.

"YES!" London says again. Actually, she shouts.

I turn to Olivia with eyebrows raised. "You know someone in a band? What are you talking about?!"

Olivia's shoulders slump at my tone. "I mean, they're not famous or anything," she mumbles.

I feel bad for making *her* feel bad, but it looks like both my besties are living in a fantasy world right now. "So, are they a bunch of moms and dads singing at a henna party?"

"Ooooh, a henna party!" London begins.

I groan. "Focus, London!"

"Sorry. Continue, Olivia. Which band do you know?"

Olivia is definitely regretting saying anything right now. She glances at the door like she wants to run away. Finally, she whispers, "Jake and his friend."

"Jake and His Friend?" I repeat. "Never heard of them."

"Maybe they're British," London says hopefully. "British bands are very cool."

"Well, their choice of names isn't the greatest," I reply.

Olivia gives us both a glare. "No, silly, my brother, Jake. He and his friend Adam—he's our neighbor—play music in the garage. They've got instruments and everything. They even write their own songs."

There is total silence as we digest this information. Jake and his friend have a band? With instruments? I doubt that London was thinking of Olivia's goofy teenage brother and his equally goofy friend when she asked the universe for a band.

But we have absolutely zero other options at this point. "Are they any good?" I ask.

Olivia shrugs. "They're okay, I guess. They just started, so . . . ?"

London is grinning by now. "It doesn't matter. We'll audition them."

CHAPTER 9

Before I can find a hundred things wrong with this plan, Dada Jee calls me to help in the kitchen. It's almost lunchtime, and Amir is throwing another tantrum. I can hear him shouting about candy.

"I gotta go," I tell my friends. "Candy denial is brutal."

"Poor baby," Olivia croons. "Just give him what he's asking for."

My eyes bug out. "You know nothing about little kids, do you?"

She shrugs happily. "Nope. I'm the youngest in my family."

"With an older brother who's in a band," London points out.

I sigh. I guess she's not letting this go. We decide to meet at Olivia's after lunch, to see if Jake and his friend are good enough for our neighborhood street party. "He'll be great!" Olivia says.

"We'll see," London says. "I'm going to make up a three-point scoring chart. Do you have blindfolds, Imaan?"

I stop at the door. "Why would I . . . ?"

"I was thinking of a blind audition," she explains. "But, forget it. No need to make it complicated."

I shake my head and wave good-bye. They let themselves out and I head to the kitchen to deal with the candy crisis. "Okay, what's the problem, kiddo?"

Amir is in tears. It's his second-favorite way to be, after super excited. "I want candy! I don't want to eat pulao!"

Dada Jee scowls ferociously. "What are you talking about? My pulao is delicious!"

This is a very true statement. Dada Jee cooks Pakistani food for us most days, and he is really good at it. Like champion-level good. Amir has no clue how lucky we are. If it wasn't for Dada Jee, we'd have to eat Mama's bland turkey sandwiches every day.

I am so not a fan of turkey sandwiches

I take a sniff from the pot on the stove. "Yummy rice, tender chicken . . . mmm." I smile so big I feel like I'm in a commercial. But I have to sell this before Mama comes running from her home office demanding to know what all the racket is about. She works as an accountant, and she needs silence to do all that math. Or something.

Amir isn't convinced. He opens his mouth to protest. "But . . ."

"If you eat your food, I'll give you candy afterward," I say. "And you can go watch Doc for a little while."

The tears disappear like a magic trick. Wow, this kid is something else. "Can I touch the bunny rabbit?" Amir asks.

I grab plates from the cabinet and scoop some pulao for both of us. "Eat first. Then we'll see."

London and I meet in front of Olivia's house later in the afternoon. "Ready?" London asks.

"I guess," I mumble. Actually, I'm so not ready to ask my bestie's brother to sing for us, but I don't think I have a choice. I'm just praying Jake's band is okay enough to perform in public.

Also, that he actually wants to do it. The few times I've met Olivia's big brother, he seemed totally obsessed with two things: video games and soccer. I'm half wondering if Olivia made up a band just to make London happy.

Ugh, what is wrong with me? Olivia would never make up stuff.

"I'm ready," I say firmly, and ring the bell.

Olivia opens the door immediately, and she's smiling. Now I feel even worse for thinking she was lying. I smile back. She takes us upstairs to Jake's room and knocks on the door. While we wait, I hear a loud cackling sound from inside. It sounds like an old lady laughing at a bad joke but also coughing at the same time. "Who's in there?" I ask, horrified.

Olivia shrugs. "Just Pixie."

Pixie. I've heard that name before. Just then, the door opens, so I swallow my questions. "Yes?" says Jake, hardly looking up from the phone in his hand. "Watchu need?"

Now that we're here, we have no idea what we're

going to say. We should have planned this part better.

"Hi," I finally say, waving my hand weakly.

Jake puts his phone into his pocket and grins. "No animals with you girls today? Did your pet-sitting agency crack under pressure?"

"We're taking care of a rabbit client right now," London tells him in a haughty tone.

"Where is it?" He looks around. "Wait, is he an invisible rabbit?"

Wow, this guy thinks he's so funny. "My grandfather is taking care of him," I say. It took a lot of pleading, but Dada Jee finally agreed. I guess he owed me since I'd gotten Amir to eat two helpings of pulao before I left.

"We need your help," Olivia says, pushing past Jake.

"Let me guess, you lost another pet?" Jake asks, turning back into the room. He helped us a few weeks ago when our first client, Sir Teddy, escaped from my house. We'd organized a search party and Jake had convinced all his friends to join.

London and I follow Jake, so now there are four people in this small bedroom.

No Pixie, though, whoever she is.

London starts to explain what we need help with. She talks about Angie, and the Silverglen Street Party, and her dreams for the best entertainment—sorry, talent—this neighborhood has ever seen. Yup, she's being totally Miss Overboard Harrison again.

Jake takes his phone out of his pocket and starts scrolling on the screen again, like he's totally bored. "Why are you telling me all this?"

"I told them about your band!" Olivia interrupts hurriedly.

"You did what?" He's not looking at his phone anymore. I guess that means he's not bored anymore?

"Any good party needs music," Olivia says. "So, you see, we need you to play music on Saturday."

London adds, "Only you have to audition so we can make sure you're actually good."

Jake loses his easy grin and scowls. He puts his hands on his hips. "Why should I even do this?"

"Don't you want your music to be heard?" Olivia asks. Her hands are also on her hips, and even though they're years apart, they look like twins. Same blond hair. Same scowl.

He flips his hair. "Of course, I want my music to be heard. It's fantastic."

I bite my lip to stop myself from laughing. "If you say so," I say in my most serious tone. The one I use to stop Amir from throwing a tantrum.

"Well, we're giving you a chance to be heard," London tells him. "In public. By actual human beings, not the mice in your garage."

"Our garage doesn't have mice," both Olivia and Jake say together.

Yup. Twins.

Before Jake can say any more, the cackling from earlier starts up again. And it's loud. So loud I almost jump out of my skin. "Who *is* that?" I hiss, looking around.

"Pixie," Jake says, sighing. "She's supposed to be taking a nap. But she hates taking a nap."

"Sounds like Amir," I joke. But the cackling makes everything less funny, like there's an evil witch in the room.

"Exactly who is Pixie?" London demands. "There's no one here except the four of us."

Jake walks to a corner of his room where a blanket hangs over something. I realize that's where the cackling is coming from. Jake reaches over and pulls the blanket away.

And underneath sits a big metal birdcage.

And inside the cage is a small blue-and-green bird.

And it's cackling like a real person.

London and I stare. Olivia waves her hand at the cage. "Meet Pixie, Jake's parakeet."

Pixie stops cackling now that she has everyone's attention. Then she says in a voice very much like Jake's: "Hello, pretty bird!"

CHAPTER 10

Now that I think about it, Jake had told us about Pixie before. It was a week ago, when we'd brought over our kitten clients to Olivia's house for an overnight stay. We'd just never met her because it was past her bedtime.

I never knew birds had bedtimes. Plus, Jake had failed to mention it was a talking bird. "How cool!" I gush. "What else can she say?"

Olivia rolls her eyes. "Don't get him started!"

Too late. Jake's already on a roll. "She can say fifteen words and phrases. And she can do five different tricks!" he tells us, smiling proudly.

"She's the best behaved bird on the planet!"

I clap my hands in glee. "Ooh, tricks! Can we see?"

London clears her throat. "Not right now, Imaan! We're here for a reason."

I turn to her. She's standing all the way at the other end of the room, near the door. "Don't you want to see Pixie's tricks?" I ask, making a little pouty face.

"No," she replies firmly.

That's weird. She usually can't resist my pouty face. "Why not?"

"The party?" she says impatiently. "Jake, can you play music at the party, pretty please?"

"Pretty bird!" Pixie shouts from the cage.

I giggle. This is going to be fun!

Jake opens the cage and puts his hand up sideways. Pixie waddles over to him and steps onto his finger. Her claws are so tiny and cute, and her head tilts to the side as she looks at Jake. "Hello, Pixie!" he croons.

My eyes pop. I never thought I'd see Olivia's teenage brother crooning to a bird.

"Hello, Pixie!" the bird repeats. "Welcome to my house!"

"Thank you, Pixie!" I tell her. Then I turn to Jake. "Tell us about her tricks."

He runs a finger over Pixie's head. "The usual stuff. Walk on a plank, climb up and down a ladder, go through a tunnel, et cetera, et cetera!"

"You taught her all those tricks?" I whisper, very impressed. Here I was, thinking Jake was a typical teenager playing video games all day. But he's in a band and he trains a bird to do all kinds of fantastic tricks. I bet he's a straight A student too!

Jake shrugs like it's no big deal. "Yeah, she's my friend." He kisses Pixie on the head.

Cuteness overload!

Pixie nuzzles his face. "Hello, friend!"

I break out into a grin. "She's so smart!" I say. "Right, London?"

London smiles a little too. "I guess." But her body language is screaming *Stay away!*

I'm not exactly sure what's going on. London's never been less than 100 percent excited about animals. That's why we started Must Love Pets. "You guess?" I ask, my grin fading.

She looks at Jake instead of me. "Listen, Jake. We really need to have music at this party. Can you please say yes?"

Jake stroked Pixie's head. "I thought you wanted an audition?" he teases.

London shakes her head. "I think we can skip that. It's not like there are multiple bands dying to play at our street party."

"You never know," I joke. "Maybe the teenagers next door also have a band."

"Sorry," Jake replies. "There's only us. Me and Adam."

He's talking about Adam Herrera, the kid whose parents are on TV. His mom is the news anchor for Channel 19, always dressed in beautiful suits and a perfect hairstyle. His dad is a writer of some kind. He was being interviewed on TV recently—not on Channel 19 obviously, that would be weird—and Dada Jee had listened with close attention because he thought anyone on TV was a celebrity.

I doubt that authors can be considered celebrities, but what do I know?

"You're in a band with the rich kid?" I ask. Now I'm thinking maybe this is a mistake. Maybe Jake and Adam don't really have any singing chops.

"You have something against rich people?" Jake asks, raising an eyebrow.

"Er, no . . ." I blink. "I just meant . . . maybe we should at least listen to them sing once."

London nods, but she's staring at Pixie the whole time. "Good idea."

Jake groans, but he nods too. "Sure. We're going to practice in Adam's garage after dinner. You can come watch."

I squeal and jump a little. "Yayy!" Attending band practice with two teenage boys? Sounds sweet!

"Hip hip hooray!" Pixie shouts.

After dinner, we assemble in Adam Herrera's garage. He's tall, with black hair and brown eyes. "Hey," he says quietly to us, before taking a guitar and slinging it across his chest.

"Hi, Adam," London replies, all businesslike. "Did Jake tell you why we're here?"

"Relax," Jake says. He's standing in front of an electronic keyboard. "We discussed it."

"And?"

"It's cool. We'd love to help you out." Adam gives us a small smile, although he doesn't really meet our eyes. I'm guessing he's shy. And very kind to help his bandmate's sister's friends for no reason.

Okay, my stereotype of rich kids is officially shattered.

Olivia leads us to an old leather couch in the corner of the garage. We sit down, giggling and whispering, and wait.

And wait.

Apparently playing in a band includes a lot of time spent tuning the equipment. And shuffling papers around. And clearing throats. Soon, my foot is tapping on the floor and I'm starting to get annoyed. We need to get back home to Doc. It's not nice to leave our client alone for so long, especially with Amir on the loose.

Finally, the boys start playing. I lean forward, my hands clasped in front of me. I fully expect it to be awesome, but it's not. Only it's not terrible either. They're singing a song by some rock band I've heard on the radio, but the words are all garbled up, and the noise from the guitar is . . . loud. I want to cover my ears with my hands, but I think that would be rude.

Maybe waiting was better.

"Well?" Jake asks when they finish.

"Well," London replies, pursing her lips.

I nudge her with my elbow. "It was great!" I say weakly. "But do you have something slower? Maybe less . . . loud?"

"Yeah, there will be kids there," Olivia adds. "So maybe something appropriate for them?"

The boys whisper to each other, then start on a new song. Immediately, I relax. This one is nice and slow, and very sweet. I grin. They're singing "Twinkle, Twinkle, Little Star," but they've totally made it their own version. It's almost like Star is some girl's name and they're telling her how beautiful she is.

Cheesy, right?

Right.

I look at my friends. London and Olivia are grinning too. "Perfect!" I cry when the boys finish. Star could totally be a girl you'd sing songs about.

Jake and Adam grin too. "Yeah?" Adam asks shyly.

London gets up from the couch and walks over to them. She places a street party flyer on the keyboard in front of Jake. "We'll redo the poster and put your band as the main act," she tells them.

The boys' grins widen, like they can't believe they'll be on an actual poster. "That's awesome!" Jake says. "We'll practice all the kids' songs we know."

"Yeah, like 'The Wheels on the Bus,' maybe?" Adam says. "We could make it really edgy."

I'm not sure what that means, but it sounds good. I somehow have faith in these boys now that I've heard them perform. Seems like London was right about holding an audition.

Jake snaps his fingers. "'Old MacDonald'! I loved that song as a kid!"

They start calling out song names, laughing and nudging each other. I roll my eyes, but it's funny too.

When they run out of ideas, they go back to their instruments. Adam strums on his guitar, and Jake runs a hand over the keyboard. The throat clearing begins again.

I guess that's our cue to leave.

"Bye, guys," Olivia says. "Thank you for doing this for Angie."

"No problem," Adam replies. "Tasty is our favorite."

We get ready to leave. At the last minute, London turns back and asks, "I forgot, what's your band's name?"

"The Silverglens," Adam replies, blushing.

Their band name is also the neighborhood name? "Perfection," I squeal.

CHAPTER 11

We're sitting cross-legged on the floor of our Pet Room the next morning when Jake rushes in. "You girls have to help me!" he says, all stressed out.

"Hush!" I hiss immediately. "You'll scare Doc."

It's true. Doc is scampering inside his big fabric tunnel, but he'll be out any second and Jake's loud voice will probably scare him silly.

"What are you doing?" Jake asks.

"Training our new client," Olivia replies. She points to the obstacle course Sonya left us. It's spread out exactly the way she showed us, waiting for Doc to pass through. "He's a genius, that rabbit."

Doc seems to hear the compliment. He peeks out of the tunnel, his nose twitching. I lean forward and offer him a sprig of cilantro. He nibbles on it like the cutie pie he is. "Good job, baby!" I whisper, running a gentle finger over one floppy ear.

"Pretty bird! Come here, pretty bird!"

No way! London, Olivia, and I swivel at the cackling sound like we're puppets on the same string. "Pixie!" I cry, finally noticing the cage Jake is holding. I start to scramble to my feet.

A movement stops me. I look down. Doc is freaking out. He hops around and tries to dash to safety, but he keeps bumping into the items on the obstacle course. I lean over and grab him before he hurts himself. "Poor baby," I whisper. His whole body is trembling. "It's only Pixie. She's harmless."

London makes a noise in her throat. "Really?" she demands. "Is Pixie harmless?"

Jake looks offended. "Of course! She'd never hurt you." Then he looks at the rabbit in my arms. "Rabbits, I'm not so sure. Who knows?"

Olivia stands up too. She crosses her arms over her chest. "What do you want, Jake? And why is the bird here?"

Jake puts the cage down on the floor as far away from Doc as possible. "Isn't it obvious?" he asks. "You're pet sitters. I have a pet. One plus one equals two."

"No need for a math lesson," Olivia replies.

He sighs. "Look, I need you to look after Pixie while Adam and I practice our songs."

I'm about to scream *yes*, but London beats me to it. "Absolutely not!" she says firmly.

Wait, what? I take Doc over to the playpen and put

him down. He immediately hops over to his carrier and disappears inside. "London," I say. "Let's find out what's going on first. Jake's never needed us to take care of Pixie before."

"I don't care. We can't just start pet sitting all the neighborhood pets for no reason."

I stare at her because she's not making sense. "Our business literally is all about taking care of pets when their owners need it."

"Not Pixie," she says.

"Why not?" Olivia, Jake, and I ask together.

There's no reply. London just looks . . . stubborn. I would try to figure out what the problem is, but we don't have time. Doc is freaking out, and Jake looks ready to yell at us. I step closer to Pixie's cage and ask Jake again: "Can you tell us what happened? Why do you need us to take care of your bird?"

He runs a frustrated hand over his hair. "She hates

it when we play music. She gets all loud and starts squawking, and rams her head against her cage. I don't want her in my room when we play."

"What happened to the garage?"

He shrugs. "It's too hot there during the day. We're practicing in my room."

This makes sense. California in the middle of summer is brutal. "Why don't you practice in Adam's room?" London asks.

He shrugs again. "His mom has a migraine. She kicked us out."

It's clear to me. If we want the Silverglens to practice for Saturday, we need to keep Pixie with us, no matter how strange London is acting. "Okay," I say. "We'll do it."

London starts to protest, but I give her a nudge in her side. "Sure, fine," she grunts.

Jake heaves a sigh of relief. "Phew, good!" He

turns around to go, but then stops. "Don't think I'm paying you. Consider it a thank-you for playing at your party."

"Of course," I say politely.

"We're very grateful," Olivia adds in a sarcastic tone.

London just stares at him until he grins and leaves.

And we're left standing in the Pet Room with a scared little rabbit and a loud parakeet.

"I don't like this," London tells us.

She's standing near Pixie's cage, glaring at the bird like it is her mortal enemy. Jake's been gone for half an hour, and we've been debating what to do the entire time. Doc still hasn't emerged from his carrier, so his training is on hold. I can hear Amir and Dada Jee talking loudly in the living room, which doesn't help the noise level much.

Plus, Pixie keeps calling out random phrases in her cackling voice, like she's trying to get us to play with her. "Pretty bird! Come here! What're you doing? Who's a pretty bird?"

We are definitely a noisy bunch. I wonder how Mama ever gets any work done, even if her office is all the way in the back of the house.

I finally decide to do something instead of just standing around. I open Pixie's cage and place my hand sideways in front of the door, like Jake did the day before. "Come on, then," I whisper to Pixie. "Come out, pretty bird."

"Ack! What are you doing?" London squawks, taking a few steps back.

I don't turn around, even though I'm irritated. "What do you have against Pixie?" I ask, but my tone is soft. If there's anything I've learned from this pet-sitting business, it's that animals understand tone. If you don't want an animal to freak out, you have to stay calm.

London is the opposite of calm right now. "Nothing!" she says shakily. "But I don't think you should let the bird out. You don't know anything about it. It could be dangerous."

Now I do turn and look at her. "Dangerous? It's literally tiny, London."

"Yes, but it has claws. And wings."

Pixie steps out of her cage and onto my finger. I try to stay still because this is the most awesome thing I could have imagined. Her little claws press into my finger, and she balances until she's steady.

A bird. Is balancing. On my hand.

I want to squeal, but I don't. Barely.

Olivia moves to stand right next to me. "Yeah, it's no big deal. Pixie's a darling." She stretches a hand to take her. I resist, but she adds, "It's okay, Pixie knows me best."

I keep my hand steady. "I know, but I got her." Ugh, I sound whiny, but I can't help it. I want Pixie to stay on my finger. I want her to talk to me and let me pet her. "You can hold her anytime, Olivia. She lives in your house."

"That's true. But Jake doesn't like me touching her. He says I'm too hyper."

I don't say anything. I turn a little away from her, and she leans forward, putting a sideways hand next to mine. "Come, Pixie!"

"Stop, Olivia!"

"OMG, why are you fighting!" London yells.

"Hush, little baby!" Pixie yells. She starts to flap her wings over and over. The movement is so quick it sounds almost like buzzing.

London lets out a screech.

That does it. Pixie takes off from my finger and flies toward the ceiling fan. I thank the universe that the fan isn't on because that would spell disaster. "Pixie, come back!" I say in what I hope is a calm voice.

Pixie doesn't listen. She flies over Olivia and then me, making loops in the air. Then she flies straight for London, her wings a blur.

"ACK!" London screeches even louder. Plus, she flaps her arms wildly around her head. "Get her away from me! Get her away!"

Yeah, this is the opposite of calm.

CHAPTER 12

Mama runs into the room, with Amir and Dada Jee close behind her. "Is everything okay?" she asks, out of breath.

The three of us are too busy to reply.

London is hiding behind the curtain, peeking out with wide eyes. Olivia is trying to catch Pixie, hissing, "Here, birdie, it's Aunt Olivia, come here!" Pixie flies around in circles near the ceiling, totally ignoring her aunt.

Me? I'm standing in the playpen, searching for Doc. Sonya told us that rabbits are prey animals, which means they get scared very easily. I'm not sure what happens to rabbits if they get too scared, but I don't want to find out.

It's not good that I can't find Doc anywhere. I suspect he's hiding in the hay in his litter box, but that is full of poop, so I'm not putting my hand in for any price. Ew.

"What's going on?" Mama asks, louder this time.

"Mama, look, a birdie!" Amir announces, pointing.

"I can see that. Imaan, I didn't know you girls took on another client." Mama doesn't sound happy at all. "I thought we agreed one client at a time."

"Pixie isn't a client!" London calls out from behind the curtain. "He was foisted on us by Olivia's big brother. We didn't have a choice."

Foisted? What does that even mean?

Mama turns to London. "Why are you hiding, dear?"

I stare at London. She reminds me of Doc, hiding at the sound of loud noises. Then it dawns on me. "Are you . . . scared of Pixie?" I ask her breathlessly. That can't be right. Pixie is a tiny parakeet, and London is . . . London. I've never known her to be scared of anything, not even when we watched a scary movie marathon last Halloween.

London is quiet. Dada Jee clears his throat and says gruffly, "It's all right. My sister used to be scared of birds too. She'd run back in the house whenever one came too close to us in the village."

"I'm not scared of birds," London protests. "I just don't like them."

Still, she's totally behind the curtain. Only her sneakers and the bottoms of her jeans are visible. I suddenly remember all the times London tensed up near the pigeons in our neighborhood park. She'd always call them a nuisance, but maybe she was scared of them?

I feel so bad. How did I not know about this? "Are you okay?" I ask softly.

The curtain moves, so I'm guessing she's either nodding or shaking her head. Ugh, not helpful. Then she whispers, "I'm fine."

"Birds can be intimidating," Mama agrees. "Flying about, dropping on you."

Dropping? Wait, does she mean poop? Pixie flies over my head just then, and we all duck like scaredy-cats. "Don't you dare poop on us!" I tell her sternly.

Pixie squawks and lands on the ceiling fan. "Go to sleep, Pixie," she cackles.

That makes Amir laugh. "I want to hold the birdie," he tells me, raising his hands high.

"She's busy right now, buddy," I reply.

"No fair!" he says, pouting. I ruffle his hair and he perks up. "What about Doc? Can I hold him?"

I laugh a little. "Let's hope he comes out to play soon."

"Pixie will stay put up there for a little while," Olivia says. "She sometimes takes a nap on the fan in Jake's room when he lets her out."

I heave a sigh of relief. "Okay, that's good." I stride to the curtain and push it aside. "London, come out now, please?"

London walks out with a sheepish smile. "Sorry for freaking out."

I hug her. "It's okay. We all have things we don't like."

"Why don't you like birds?" Amir asks, eyes big and honest. I like how he can just say whatever he's feeling.

London shrugs. "Once when I was little, a tiny bird flew into my hair. It was so creepy." She shudders. "I could feel its wings against my head. I've hated them ever since. Stupid things."

I hug her even tighter. "OMG, that sounds horrible. When did this happen? Why didn't I know?"

She holds on to me. "It happened at my grandma's place in Connecticut one summer. I just wanted to forget about it when I got home."

Dada Jee clears his throat again. "How about some lemonade, huh, brave girl?"

London lets go of me. "That sounds like a great idea. Lead the way, Dada Jee!"

I smile at her using my Urdu name for my grandfather. "Leave some for me!" I call out as they head to the kitchen with Amir between them.

Mama looks at us, then at Pixie on the fan. "Should I ask why you girls even have this bird?"

Olivia and I explain about the Tasty street party, Jake's band, and Adam's mom's migraine. Mama's face gets more and more pinched as we talk. "You girls are biting off more than you can chew," she warns.

I happen to agree with her, but not about the band. It's a good thing she doesn't know about London's talent list.

"It's for a good cause," I remind her cheerfully. "Angie is a neighbor, right, Mama? And we always help our neighbors." She's given me this lecture a hundred times.

"I should never have told you about your neighborly duties," she grumbles, but she's smiling a little. I know she's proud of me for being so responsible. "Just . . . if that bird poops all over the room, you girls will be in trouble!"

Gross. I look up quickly, but Pixie has her head tucked into her wing now. She looks completely harmless, as if she hasn't spent the last fifteen minutes flying about like a possessed bird.

"We'll get her back in her cage ASAP!" Olivia promises.

Things get back to normal by late afternoon. Jake returns from his practice and isn't the least bit surprised to find Pixie on the ceiling fan. He snaps his fingers and calls her, and she flies to his finger like it's no big deal.

"Why didn't she listen to me?" Olivia moans.

"Because you're too hyper," he replies, grinning. "All you girls are."

I don't even try to protest. The scene in this room a couple of hours ago was pretty wild. Jake puts Pixie back in her cage and waves good-bye to us. "Same time tomorrow," he calls as he leaves.

"Ugh," London says from the doorway. She'd come back from her lemonade break a while ago, but she'd stayed at the edge of the room. I'm guessing she wants to keep as far away from the ceiling fan as possible.

We hang out on the floor, watching Bugs Bunny

cartoons on my laptop. London and Olivia were right, this Bugs character is hilarious. Also, more than a little scary. I wouldn't want to be on his bad side.

Soon, Doc comes out of his litter box and allows me to pick him up. "I missed you, baby," I whisper in his floppy ear. He twitches his nose like he's saying hello.

"Let's finish the training," Olivia says.

We sit on the floor and watch as Doc goes through the items one by one. The fence, the slide, the fabric tunnel . . . he jumps and crawls and squeezes through. Olivia feeds him treats at every turn, and he quickly reaches the end. "Good job!" we all whisper-shout.

"He's a pro!" London adds. I want to hug her. She looks her usual, happy self now that no birds are nearby.

"He really is." I sigh.

There's a pause, then London says slowly, "We should bring Doc to the street party."

"Of course, we'll need to bring him with us," says Olivia. "We'll be out there all day, and we can't leave him here alone."

She shakes her head. "I meant, bring him as an act," London explains.

"We can't . . ." I sputter. "He's a client . . . that would be . . ."

"We could ask Sonya," London says. "I bet she'd say yes. She's trained him to perform in front of people, right?"

I put my hand out like a stop sign. "You're not thinking clearly. You're just freaked out about what happened earlier."

"What happened earlier?" London asks in a tough voice.

Okay, I guess we're going to pretend that she didn't freak out over a bird. "Nothing . . ."

"Then you have to agree my plan is great!"

I sigh and start chewing on my lip. "I don't know, London. Angie never asked for this." The three of us bringing a half-trained rabbit to a street party with a big crowd and music? What could possibly go wrong?

Olivia claps her hands so loudly I jump. "I think it's a great idea!" she says.

"You do?" I'm pretty sure my eyes are popping out of my head. How can anyone think this is a good idea?

Olivia nods. "Let's call Sonya and ask her. What's the worst that will happen?"

I can think of about a hundred things. But nobody is listening to me.

CHAPTER 13

Sonya doesn't answer the phone, so we have to wait until the next morning when she's told us she's going to visit. That means she gets to meet not only Doc but also Pixie cackling away in her cage.

"Who's this beauty?" she asks, standing in the middle of the Pet Room, hands on hips, peering into the cage.

"My brother's parakeet, Pixie," Olivia replies. "We're looking after her while he practices music."

"Music?" Sonya asks absently as she pets Pixie's feathers from between the bars of the cage. "Like for school? I thought it was summer break."

"Oh no, he's got a band."

Sonya turns her head, eyebrows raised. "Wow, kids in this neighborhood are cool."

I'm not sure if she's joking, but I laugh anyway.

"Jake's not cool," Olivia says firmly.

I think he is, but I keep quiet.

Pixie flaps her wings. "Hello, Pixie! Welcome to my house!"

Sonya smiles. "Nice to meet you, Pixie!" She reaches over to open Pixie's cage like she's done it a thousand times. I swallow nervously. There's no way I want a repeat performance of the day before, when Pixie flew around the room and London hid behind the curtain.

"Uh, don't you want to see Doc?" I quickly ask.

Sonya turns around. "Oh yes, how is he behaving?" She abandons Pixie's cage and heads over to the playpen. Doc is sitting in the middle of the pen, eating hay. She climbs inside and sits on the blankets next to him. "Hello, buddy, did you miss me?"

I think she's the one missing all her animals. I couldn't imagine going from an office space full of them to being totally alone. "He's been good," I say in my most customer service tone. "You don't have to worry about him."

She waits quietly. After a few minutes, Doc leaves the hay and hops onto her lap. She leans forward until their noses touch. It's like they're in their own little world.

"Aw, that's adorable!" I whisper.

London clears her throat. "Doc's training is going really well," she says. I guess she's building up courage to ask permission to include Doc in the street party. I still think it's a bad idea, but I'm waiting for Sonya to shut it down.

"I'm so proud of you, buddy!" Sonya whispers to him. "You're going to be a great performer!"

"We think so too!" London says. "That's why we were hoping you'd allow him to show off tricks at our neighborhood street party this weekend. He'll be so great, and the kids will absolutely love him!"

Way to go, buttering up the client, London!

I'm waiting for Sonya to say no, to get mad or laugh, or something. Anything. But she doesn't say anything. She keeps touching noses with Doc until I think maybe she forgot London was talking to her. "I think that's a good idea," she finally murmurs.

What? How is this a good idea? Isn't she worried for her pet?

I guess we must all be staring at her in shock because Sonya starts to smile. "It's good practice for him to do the obstacle course in front of a crowd. That's what he'll be doing soon anyway at birthday parties and things."

I had not realized Doc would be performing tricks for people like a real job. "Do you think he's ready?" I ask.

Sonya smiles some more. "Only one way to find out, right?"

She stays for another half hour, and we go through Doc's entire obstacle course three times in front of her. "He's definitely ready," Sonya finally announces.

"Yup," London and Olivia say.

I sigh, because I still think it's a bad idea.

After Sonya leaves, the three of us head to the kitchen in search of snacks. Dada Jee is sitting at the kitchen table with our neighbor Mr. Greene, drinking lemonade. "You have to give me this recipe," Mr. Greene says. "It's amazing."

It's funny, because Mr. Greene asks Dada Jee for the recipe almost every day. Dada Jee always ignores him. "Come to the farmers' market next week and buy a gallon or two," Dada Jee says.

I take a bag of chips from the pantry and dump it into a big bowl. London slides into a chair and pours herself a glass of lemonade. "Or you should come to the street party on Saturday, Mr. Greene. There will be lots of things to eat and drink."

Mr. Greene frowns like he's never heard of a street party before. So London, Olivia, and I take turns explaining it to him as we munch on chips. "Sounds chaotic," he finally pronounces with a slightly horrified look on his face. I don't blame him. He lives alone and is usually even more grumpy than Dada Jee.

"Not at all," London says "It'll be loads of fun." Then she gets that look on her face again, the one that means another grand idea is coming. "I know! You could showcase some of your art there. Get publicity for your Etsy store."

"I could?"

She tells him all about the tables for local businesses. Mr. Greene listens thoughtfully. "You've got a good head for business, young lady," he says.

London smiles like it's the best compliment anyone

has ever given her. "So should I add you to my talent list?"

"Most definitely!"

We say good-bye to Mr. Greene and Dada Jee, and head back to the Pet Room to get Pixie. We'll be bringing her to Olivia's house since we're eating lunch there. London stays very far away from the cage, eyeing Pixie carefully as we walk across the street. "You okay?" I ask her. I'm still not over how scared she was when Pixie escaped.

London gives me a brave smile. "Fine."

I decide not to ask again. She hates looking cowardly.

We're sitting at the Gordons' dining table eating grilled cheese sandwiches and the most delicious strawberry salad ever, when Mr. Gordon peeks in. "Oh good, you girls are here! I wanted to talk to you."

He's got a serious look on his face, so I'm guessing it's not good news.

"What is it, Dad?" Olivia asks.

He comes inside and scratches his head. "Um, I got a call from my manager this morning. I've got to work on Saturday because one of the other guys broke his arm."

I want to be sad for the other guy's arm, I really do. But mostly I'm worried about London and her unstoppable search for talent. What will she do now that Mr. Gordon is out?

"Oh, Dad, it's okay," Olivia says. She gets up and hugs him. "Don't feel bad. I hope your friend feels better soon."

"Yeah, well, I'm sorry for letting you down." He's looking pretty upset.

"We understand," I say quickly. "It's not like you said yes for sure. We didn't put you down as a definite, right, London?"

London doesn't say anything, so I kick her under the

table. "It's okay, right, London? We have a performing rabbit now, so it evens out."

London kicks me back but not too hard. "Sure, it's fine," she finally says. "Don't worry, Mr. Gordon."

He looks relieved. "Good. Glad you girls understand." He turns to leave, then says, "It's not like I'm very good at those pictures anyway. Olivia is the real talent in this family."

He winks at his daughter, and she blushes a little. "Thanks, Dad."

We're deathly quiet once Mr. Gordon leaves the room. Olivia's blush has faded, and now she just looks pale. London is scowling at her clipboard. I bite my lip. We have an Etsy store and a rabbit on the list, but we lost caricatures. Honestly, I'm fine with these changes. This street party is supposed to be fun, not a whole lot of stress.

Then London looks up, and I see her clearly. Her face is the literal definition of stress.

CHAPTER 14

We finish lunch in silence, then take our plates back into the kitchen. Olivia's mom is at the grocery store, so it's our job to wash the dishes and leave the kitchen clean. Olivia hands us mini ice-cream cones from the freezer, and we trudge upstairs to her bedroom quietly. Chocolate chip is usually my favorite, but right now it's got zero taste.

Silently, we stand around the room and look at one another. There's a colorful rug in the middle and lots of throw cushions on the side near one wall. The room is a little messy, so I swallow the last of my cone and start picking things up from the floor.

"You don't have to do that," Olivia says, startled.

I keep going. "Sorry, it's a habit with me. I try to help Mama as much as I can." I give her a quick smile. "It's not a problem, I don't mind."

It really isn't. There are just a few clothes and socks lying around. I put everything in a neat pile on the chair near the bed. "There," I say, patting the jeans on the top.

"Wanna have a conversation, Imaan?" London says dryly.

I nod. "Sure. Let's talk."

London looks at her clipboard again. "So, Mr. Gordon is out," she says.

"It's not a big deal," Olivia replies with a shrug. "We have plenty of other things going on at the party."

This is true.

Still, I look at London because she's the one deciding the talent. "Well?"

London purses her lips as she looks at her list. I can almost see the wheels turning in her brain. After about thirty seconds, she looks straight at Olivia. "You should replace your dad," she says firmly.

My mouth drops open.

Olivia gasps. "What are you talking about? I can't draw caricatures."

"No, but your dad said you're the most talented in your family." She points a finger at Olivia. "You, not him. Not even Jake."

"Jake is talented . . ." I start, but both my friends give me eye rolls, so I stop talking. Maybe this is not the right time to talk about my bestie's teen musician brother.

"I can't draw," Olivia says again, louder, like she's trying to convince everyone. She's correct, because I've seen her art on the flyers we made for Must Love Pets and it's not spectacular.

"I'm not talking about drawing," London replies, eyebrows waggling.

"What are you talking about, then?"

I look at London, and suddenly I know exactly what she's hinting at. "Your camera!" I say excitedly. "That's your talent, Olivia! Of course it is!"

London nods. We've been trying to convince Olivia to show her pictures to the outside world, but she's so shy and never thinks they're any good. It's totally false, though, because she's a wizard with a camera. Some of her pictures are currently in Mr. Greene's Etsy store as part of his Everyday Nature collection. Actual people could be looking at them online right now, maybe even buying them with actual money.

Cool, right?

Right.

Olivia obviously doesn't agree because she's shaking her head. "No, that's ridiculous! I'm not displaying pictures. Mr. Greene is already doing that. We don't need two people doing the same thing."

"Why not?" I ask, warming up to this idea very quickly. That's me, Imaan On Board.

Olivia gives me an annoyed look. "It's against the principles of business, right?" she asks London. "You can't have two businesses with the same products too close together or something?"

London nods slowly. "It's called market cannibalization."

"Market what?" I ask. Sounds gross.

"It's like eating your own species. Some snakes do that."

Definitely gross. "Okay, so no cannibals at the street party," I joke, trying to clear the air. "Any other ideas? Personally, I think we don't really need another act. We have enough talent, don't we?"

London isn't even listening. "Why don't you

want to display your pictures, Olivia? You could join Mr. Greene's table. He wouldn't mind."

Olivia puts her hands on her hips. "What else? Want me to dance a jig? Play a clown?"

"Oooh . . ." I begin.

"NO!" both my besties tell me sharply.

"Sorry!" I grin. I can't imagine what they have against a clown or two. They're hilarious.

London and Olivia go back to ignoring me. They're literally standing toe-to-toe now, scowling and grumpy. I think they've spent too much time with Dada Jee and Mr. Greene lately.

"Why are you so scared of showing your talent to everyone?" London demands. "What's the problem? Don't you think you're good enough? Because let me tell you right now, you're great! Your pictures are awesome! If you can't see that, you're . . . you're an ostrich burying your head in the sand!"

I totally agree with the awesome part. But the way London speaks, it doesn't really sound like a compliment. Calling our friend an ostrich isn't going to help her be more confident.

Olivia gasps again. "I'm not an ostrich! They have wings! You can't hold a camera with wings."

London rolls her eyes very hard. "You know what I mean. It's metaphorical."

"Another big word, London?" Olivia hisses. "We all know how smart you are!"

"That's right, I'm supersmart!"

"We're fifth graders! Not businesswomen on *Shark Tank*!" Olivia throws up her hands.

"They have kids on *Shark Tank* all the time!"

Okay, I've had enough. I step between the two angry bears, AKA my besties, and put my hands up like a traffic cop. "STOP!"

They ignore me. "Don't say anything against my

favorite TV show!" London tells Olivia angrily.

"Don't say anything about my pictures," Olivia replies, also angrily.

"I said stop fighting!" I cry. "What is wrong with you two?"

"She started it!" they both shout together.

I sigh heavily. "Let's all calm down. Olivia, *Shark Tank* is the best, and you know it. London, we can't force Olivia to do anything she doesn't want to do."

London scowls some more. "Why are you so scared, Olivia?" she asks harshly.

Olivia narrows her eyes. "Scared?" she repeats, in a really fearsome low voice. "I'm not scared."

London shrugs. "Seems like it to me."

I can't believe it. London is actually trying to make this fight worse. What is wrong with her? She's usually so calm and collected, I'm not sure what she's thinking. Does she want to make Olivia lose her temper?

I look at my best friends. They're breathing heavily and glaring at each other like total enemies. This is bad.

Olivia steps closer until she's right up to London's face. I try not to yelp since I'm squeezed between the two of them like a filling in the worst sandwich ever.

"You're the one who's scared," Olivia says very quietly. "Scared of a little bird."

We all freeze.

I gulp. This is more than bad. This is catastrophic.

I'm no longer Jokey Imaan. I've got to turn into Mama Imaan and save these two from becoming the worst kind of enemies. I fling into action. I grab Olivia by the arm and drag her away to her bed. "Sit down!" I tell her. I point my finger to let her know I'm serious.

Then I turn to London. Her face has fallen, and she looks . . . heartbroken. I clasp her in a tight sideways hug. "It's okay, Olivia didn't mean it."

"No, she's right," London whispers. "I'm scared of a little bird. What's wrong with me?"

Olivia flops down on the bed with an arm over her eyes. "OMG, I'm *so* sorry. I'm a horrible friend; what's wrong with me?"

I roll my eyes and let London go. "Okay, you drama queens. We need to talk about this."

London shakes her head. "What's there to talk about? I've got a bird phobia. I freak out when I get close to something that's smaller than my head."

"Everybody has fears," I tell her. "I think that's what Olivia was trying to say, even though she did a horrible job of it."

"Thanks," Olivia croaks.

I continue. "Olivia was saying that just like you've got a fear that doesn't make sense, she does too. Only hers is about her photography."

London looks up. "That actually makes sense."

Phew. "Maybe we can help one another get over our fears?" I say. "Slowly? Patiently?"

Olivia sits up and gives a shaky smile. "I think that's a great idea."

London nods too. "Yeah."

I let my breath out in a whoosh. There's only so much drama I can take per day. I open up my arms wide. "Three-way hug?"

CHAPTER 15

We end up with zero hugs but plenty of small, *I'm sorry* smiles. I don't mind. It will definitely take some time to get back to normal after a fight, even with three besties.

London and Olivia may not be fighting anymore, but they sure are grumpy around each other. They arrive at my place bright and early on Friday morning, and we work on party prep. There are so many last-minute things to take care of, it's not even funny.

Who thought planning a street party would be easy while we're also pet sitting not one but two animals?

London, that's who. The person who's currently

sitting on the beanbag chair in my room, staring at her clipboard with an annoyed look on her face. "We only have one fire truck," she complains.

Olivia, who's sprawled out on the shaggy carpet, rolls her eyes. "How many did you want, London?"

"One fire truck is enough, of course," London says, rolling her eyes the same way. "But I was hoping for a police car too. Kids love sitting in the back of a police car!"

"Well, we don't always get what we want, do we?"

I sit up on my bed and grit my teeth. Even though both girls are talking in sugary-sweet voices, I know they're still sort of mad at each other. Or at least hurt. I'm not sure.

What I am sure about is that if they don't resolve their issues soon, the street party is going to be a big failure. "We have to work together, guys," I say.

They both turn to look at me. "What are you talking about? Of course, we're working together." Olivia bats her eyelashes.

"Yeah, it's called brainstorming," London agrees.

"Listen to her, she knows all the big words."

I throw a pillow at them. "Ugh, just . . . hush!"

We go back to work. Olivia's making a big flyer for Angie's store window. I've offered to help, but she says she's fine working alone. I'm watching a video on my laptop about a woman with ten pet rabbits. Apparently, they can be quite a handful when they team up.

I watch a rabbit chew through the wires of the woman's television. I'm suddenly very glad Doc is alone. I couldn't imagine two or more of him hopping around, noses twitching.

London mutters over her clipboard. I look up. "Tell me what's wrong," I say.

"Nothing, just counting the talent."

"Tell me," I insist.

She sighs and sits up. "Okay, here goes. Doc's tricks will go at the halfway point of the program.

I want to wait until we have a big crowd."

"That's a good idea," I reply. London is so good at organizing and planning.

"And the last item on the agenda is the band, of course."

"Like a grand finale," I say.

"Exactly."

"Can you get to the problem?" Olivia asks from the carpet. I didn't know she was listening.

London throws her an annoyed look, then goes back to her clipboard. "We need something to entertain the kids while the adults go around sampling the food and drinks."

"The fire truck won't be enough for them?" Olivia asks in a snarky tone.

I tell myself to have some patience. They love each other, they're just mad right now. It's okay, I get mad at people I love sometimes too. Then I get over it.

I just wish London and Olivia would hurry up and get over it. I'm not sure how much more snark I can take.

"The fire truck and the petting zoo will be there," London says, "but they're only big enough for one or two kids at the same time. I want something else."

Olivia sits up from the floor and snaps her fingers. "I know! We can bring Pixie along, and she can entertain the kids by talking to them."

I cringe. "Really, Olivia?"

She shrugs. "Why not?" She looks at London. "It's just an idea. Will it be a problem?"

London shakes her head. "No, actually it's a good idea. Can you ask Jake?"

"Sure. He won't mind."

They sound like strangers, not best friends. I wait for fireworks, but nothing happens. Maybe they're really okay with each other now. "Good, glad that's settled." I smile at both of them and go back to my laptop.

"As long as London doesn't start freaking out," Olivia mutters under her breath.

I sigh.

After feeding and training Doc, we head back to my room. Jake won't bring Pixie for pet sitting until after lunch, so we have some time to hang out.

Only with London and Olivia still being frosty with each other, I'm not sure what to do. "How about a game of Monopoly?" I ask.

"Too boring," Olivia replies.

She's not wrong. I love Monopoly, but it goes on forever. I play sometimes with Dada Jee, but Amir hates it so we end very quickly. "I also have Twister."

"What are we, five?" London scoffs.

I roll my eyes. "What else can we do?"

Olivia touches the Happy Meal toys on my dresser

again. She always does that, like she's fascinated with them. "You promised to show us pictures of your dad," she says suddenly.

"I did?"

"Olivia's right, you did." This is from London.

I'm so happy they're agreeing with each other that I find myself nodding and heading out the door. "Okay, then, come with me!"

London and Olivia follow. "Oooh, where are we going?" It's funny how they're speaking at the same time. It's like they're in sync.

I relax. If I have to show London and Olivia my baba's pictures to get them friendly again, it's worth it.

Plus, I love looking at Baba's face, even in grainy pictures.

"We're going into Mama's closet." We enter Mama's room and I close the door carefully behind me. "She's got a box in there with photo albums and things."

Olivia looks around the room nervously. "Are you sure your mom will be okay with this?"

"Yeah," I reply cheerfully, even though I think she might not be okay with it. Still, it's a risk I'm willing to take to make my friends happy again.

I open the closet and reach a hand to the top shelf. It's high, and I have to stand on tippy-toes. "Almost there," I grunt.

"Maybe we shouldn't . . ." London starts

My fingers close over the big cardboard box. "Got it!" I pull and the box slides forward with a jerk. There are other things crammed around it, and some of them tremble. "Come on, treasure box!" I mutter.

I pull again, and the box comes loose into my hand. I slowly bring it down, with London and Olivia helping at each side. "Wow, it's heavy," Olivia comments.

We take the box over to Mama's big bed and place it in the middle. London and Olivia look at me. I give them a reassuring grin and climb on the bed. "Come on!"

They climb on too. I open the lid and take out the big, red-velvet-covered album. "It's so fancy," Olivia whispers.

"It's a wedding album from Pakistan."

"I remember," London murmurs. She'd come over for dinner with her parents a couple of years ago, and Mama had brought out the album to show Mr. and Mrs. Harrison what weddings in Pakistan looked like.

Hint: lots of bling.

I turn the pages carefully as my friends watch. We ooh and aah over the pictures of Mama and Baba in their wedding finery. "Your mom looks so young," London says.

"It's the lighting," Olivia says slowly. "It makes the subject glow softly."

I squeeze her hand. Just like I love hearing London talk about business, I also love hearing Olivia talk about photography. It's like both my friends have these incredible talents that make them super special.

I focus on Baba's face and try not to think about how I have zero talents that make me super special. It's okay. I don't need anything.

We go through all the albums, laughing at my baby pictures and how Dada Joo looked so different as a young man. "He still looks grumpy, though," Olivia points out.

I talk about Baba and how amazing he was. I share my memories of him, how he let me ride on his back like a pony, how we played tag in the neighborhood park. I thought I'd be sad, but talking about him actually makes me really happy.

I'm grinning when we hear Amir stomping up the stairs and shouting for me. "Imaan, where are you? I wanna play with the bunny rabbit!"

"Quick, we need to put the albums back!" I scramble off the bed and lunge for the closet, box in my arms. I stand tall and shove the box back onto the shelf. Of course, it sticks. I push harder.

"Stop, Imaan, you're going to break something!" London says, panicked.

I don't listen because Amir is getting closer. If he sees us, he's going to tell Mama and I will be in deep trouble. I'm not allowed to open her closet without permission. I'm definitely never allowed to go through her treasure box without her. I thrust the box up onto the closet shelf with all my strength. But then I feel things fall from above and hear a giant crash.

I look down at the mess on the closet floor. Glass bangles are strewn around, shattered into pieces. A small glass bottle is lying on its side, perfume spilling out.

I'm doomed.

CHAPTER 16

Saturday is a fantastic day. The sky is a little cloudy, and the breeze is nice and cool.

Party prep is officially over. We've spent most of Friday taking Doc through his obstacle course about a million times. He's really awesome, looking at us with bright eyes and twitching that adorable nose. Sonya was right that he loves kids. Now that Amir stays quiet in the Pet Room, Doc hops all the way up into his lap and gets comfy. Amir feeds him treats and pets his head, grinning widely all the time.

London's called everyone on her talent list to confirm

that they're coming. And we've put up posters in the neighborhood park and on street corners. I should feel great, but I don't. The broken glass in Mama's closet haunts my dreams, even though we'd quickly cleaned everything up. Plus, London and Olivia may have forgotten their epic fight, but nothing was actually resolved.

I'm not surprised. Things like fears and stress don't just disappear in one day. Ask me—I've been feeling sad about Baba's death for years, and it's never gotten any better. In fact, the more time that passes, the more it worries me. Maybe one day, I'll forget him completely. Then I'll just be Imaan the Lonely, without a baba.

Okay, I get why Mama calls me dramatic.

Time to focus on the positives. After all, a few good things came out of the fight on Thursday. London's been trying to keep still whenever Pixie's in the room with us. She doesn't freeze or hide behind the curtains. Once Jake even took Pixie out of her cage and walked her around my house on his finger to meet Mama, Dada Jee, and Amir. London didn't freak out, although she blinked so fast I thought her eyelashes would fall off.

BTW, I count this as progress.

Also, Olivia's agreed to showcase her work at the street party today. Not with prints of her pictures like Mr. Croono, but as a photo booth operator. She's got her fancy camera connected to her home printer with Wi-Fi, and anyone who wants their picture printed out can get it later for a small fee. I really hope this will make Olivia confident about her incredible skills with a camera. Plus, I want the whole world to know how amazing she is.

I can't wait to see her in action.

We get to Tasty a little after nine o'clock in the morning. The party will start at ten, but we want to help Angie set up. Mama drives us in her car because we have so many things to carry.

The three-minute drive is quiet. I've been trying not to make eye contact with Mama since yesterday morning, when we sneaked into her room and destroyed her property. She parks outside Tasty and stares at me in the rearview mirror so hard, I'm pretty sure she knows something is wrong. "Have fun, girls," she says. "I'll swing by a little later with your grandfather and his lemonade."

We start to climb out carefully. London's got not only her clipboard but a big three-ring binder with all sorts of papers. Olivia's carrying a crate with flyers, art supplies (in case she needs to make more flyers), and her precious camera. I'm last, with Doc's carrier in one hand and Sonya's bag of obstacles in the other. "Wait, Imaan!" Mama calls from the driver's seat.

"I gotta go, Mama!" I push the door open with my leg since my arms are full.

"I just want to make sure everything is all right," she says. "You've been acting strange <u>since</u> yesterday."

Yikes, is she psychic? "I'm okay," I mutter, not looking at her. "Just stressed about the show with Doc."

"Hmm, yes, you do have a habit of biting off more than you can chew."

I turn and give her an outraged look. It's the second time she's said this, and I really don't like it.

Mama laughs a little. "But you always make things work," she adds. "It's what makes you special."

My outrage turns to shock. Then to what's probably a very happy grin. "Yeah, that's true!" I agree cheerfully. "Just call me Imaan the Fixer of Problems."

"Come on, Imaan!" London calls. I slide out of the car and push the door shut with my elbow. Mama waves at us and drives away.

"Hey, girls!" Angie greets us from under the main awning in the parking lot. We put everything down on the ground—except Doc's carrier, which stays clutched in my hands—and walk over to her.

"Wow, this already looks so great!" I tell her. I'm not even joking. There are white folding tables set up all over the parking lot in a big U shape, each with its own little tent to keep out the sun. I'm guessing these are for vendors like Angie and Dada Jee. On the fourth side of the lot, next to a small clump of trees, is a square section of the ground laid out with a gray carpet and roped off with traffic cones. I'm pretty sure this is where the live entertainment will go, like Jake and Adam's band and Doc's obstacle course.

Gulp. It means all eyes will be on us. How hadn't I thought about this before?

"It's wonderful," Angie replies. "But I have to say, I wasn't expecting all this. You girls went way beyond my expectations."

I look at her closely. That sounds like a compliment,

but you can't always be sure with adults. "Thanks," I finally say. "You can blame London for going overboard."

London scoffs, but she's smiling like she loves going overboard on everything. Which she does. "Where will the fire truck go?" she asks.

Angie points across the street, where there's an open lot between two houses. "That's for the fire truck and the animals."

Animals? I blank for a second, before remembering that Tamara from the farmers' market is going to bring some of her goats for a mini petting zoo. I jump a little in my shoes, forgetting all about my stage fright. "Do you think we'll see Marmalade?" I whisper to Olivia.

"Hope so," Olivia whispers back.

London grabs her binder and walks toward the folding tables. "Okay, get to work, ladies," she says briskly, handing us paper signs from the binder that will go on each table. Olivia finds some painter's tape in her crate, and we get to work. After all the signs are taped up on the tables, we also tape up event flyers on shop windows and clean up the ground a little. Angie brings out a big banner that says *Welcome to the First Annual Silverglen Street Party!* and one of her employees follows with a stepladder. They fix the banner to the front of Tasty's awning while London, Olivia, and I watch with round eyes.

"Perfection." I sigh when the banner is up.

London looks around. "It's almost ten o'clock. The talent should be here soon."

The first to arrive is Tamara's van with two cute little faces peeking out from the window bars. "Marmalade!" I cry, placing Doc's carrier on a table and rushing across the street.

"Careful!" Angie yells, and I slow down.

I'm panting as I help Tamara and her mom bring the goats out. I immediately recognize Marmalade from his torn ear. "I missed you, silly goat!" I tell him, flinging my arms around his neck.

Marmalade bleats and pushes his head into my stomach like he's saying he missed me too. The next minute, I'm surrounded by London and Olivia, who also want their goat hugs. We grin at one another, remembering all the wild times we had with Marmalade. "Still eating paper, my friend?" I ask him.

"He sure is," Tamara replies, shaking her head. "Yesterday he ate my science homework! I'd spent so much time on it."

"Sorry," I say with sympathy. Tamara not only goes to high school but also helps her parents with their farm. She's my inspiration.

Tamara shrugs. "It's okay. I'll redo it over the weekend. It'll be good practice."

Once the goats are tied to the truck and munching on hay, we head back to the parking lot to greet the rest of the talent. I grab Doc's carrier and peer inside. His little nose is twitching, and he stares around with big eyes. "Hello, buddy," I whisper to him through the mesh.

Obviously, he doesn't reply.

London stands nearby with her clipboard, checking people off when they arrive. There's Dada Jee with his jugs of lemonade, buckets of ice, and a bag of tiny red plastic cups. On one side of him is Mr. Bajpai with small bowls of his wife's chutneys and pita chips for dunking. On the other side, Mr. Greene is setting up picture frames. Two elderly ladies who look like sisters are laying out a series of handmade quilts, with a sign that says *Silverglen Quilters Club. Next meeting, Monday at six p.m.*

Then I spot the best table of all. The Tasty table,

piled high with samples of delicious pies, sandwiches, and of course smoothies. "Which smoothie are you serving?" Olivia asks Angie.

Angie winks. "Both of your favorites. We'll see which one wins."

I frown. "Wins?"

London grins wickedly. "We're going to ask people to vote on which flavor they like best, Strawberry Kiwi or Berry Berry Wild."

I notice a pile of index cards on the table and a mug full of pencils. "Let's see who the winner is," Olivia says, hands on hips.

"Bring it on!" I reply with my widest grin.

CHAPTER 17

It's ten o'clock when the biggest entertainment of the party—Jake and Adam—show up. London is standing at the edge of the parking lot, watching as the boys scramble out of Mrs. Gordon's van. "You were supposed to be here thirty minutes ago!"

Jake grins easily and starts to unload things from the back of the van. "Rock stars are always late."

"Rock stars . . . ?" London begins in a loud voice.

Adam walks toward us with his arms full of wires and things. "Where should we set up?" he asks quietly.

Olivia quickly takes him to the square space blocked

off by traffic cones. "Angie's employees can help with the outlets," she says.

I put Doc's carrier on an empty table in the corner and start unloading with Jake. London glares at him for a few more seconds, then sighs and helps too. With three sets of hands, it only takes one trip to take the keyboard, guitar, and microphone back to the stage area. "Don't worry," Jake tells London. "It won't take long to set everything up."

"Yeah, they're not going to start until later anyway," I add helpfully.

London's jaw is clenched, but she nods and walks away. "Good luck. I'll check in with you later."

Jake heads back to the van. "One more thing," he says. He reaches inside and grabs something covered with a blanket. Pixie's cage. "Take good care of my bird. She hates loud noises, you know."

I roll my eyes at him. "Yes, I know."

We wave good-bye to Mrs. Gordon, and I take Pixie back to my little table in the corner. I crouch to peek at Doc. I think he's gone to sleep because I can only see a ball of fur. I'm starting to get a little worried about him. I'm not sure how long you're supposed to keep rabbits inside a small space. Don't they need to hop around or something? Stretch those cute little legs?

"Whatcha doing, Imaan?"

I look over my shoulder. It's Amir, grinning. "Did you come with Dada Jee?" I ask.

He nods sadly. "He's no fun. He just wants to sell his lemonade."

I straighten up. "That's okay. You can stay with me."

Amir catches sight of Doc's carrier. "Bunny's here!" he cries, and jostles me, trying to get closer.

I put a hand on his shoulder. "Careful, Amir. You don't want Doc to get scared."

Amir pushes his face right into the mesh carrier.

"Hello, Doc," he breathes. "It's me, your best friend."

I smile a little. Amir and Doc have indeed become friendly in the last few days.

I chew on my lip. I have to do something about Pixie, pronto. It's not going to be easy handling two animals and also keep my little brother out of trouble. I look around for Olivia, but she and London are all the way at the stage, helping Jake and Adam with setup. Since it's after ten, guests have also started arriving. There are now several families with kids walking around. A few are tasting samples. Some of the adults are standing around chatting.

I hear a loud noise. A little kid is crying, trying to pull his mom away from Tasty's sample table. This means it's time for Pixie to work her magic. "Stay here and keep an eye on Doc, okay?" I say to Amir.

He gives me a salute.

I carefully pull the blanket away from the cage and

fold it up on the table. "Hello, birdie," I say, tapping the bars a little.

Pixie takes her head out of her wings and looks around with interest. "Hello, everyone! What fun we're going to have today!"

I giggle. "Definitely! You ready to charm some kids?"

"Hello, everyone!" Pixie repeats. I guess that means she's ready.

Pixie is a big hit. I take her cage over to the crying child, and he immediately dries his tears when he sees a talking bird. Pixie loudly tells everyone her name and how happy she is to be here. There are some cackling and sneezing sounds, followed by "Excuse me!" which makes the kid laugh.

Soon, there's a crowd of five or six small children

around me, all pushing to get closer to Pixie. I edge away a little, not sure how Pixie will react. At least she's in the cage, not flying outside.

Only that's not true. Olivia walks up and grins to see the kids looking at Pixie so adoringly. "Hey, you want to touch the bird?" she asks.

"I don't think that's a good idea," I whisper.

Olivia shrugs. "Jake does it all the time. Pixie loves the attention." She opens the door of the cage and holds out her hand sideways like I've seen Jake do so many times. In a flash, Pixie has stepped onto her finger, cackling, "Who's a pretty bird? Welcome, everyone!" over and over.

I guess she's happy to be out of the cage. I don't blame her. Cages are awful.

The kids ooh and aah, and jostle one another to get closer. "One at a time," Olivia says.

Only no one's listening. I watch in horror as they

all reach their grubby little hands toward Pixie at the same time, calling her name like something in a scary movie. Pixie flaps her wings and squawks loudly. "Hush, little baby!"

"She doesn't like noise, kids!" I shout, only to realize that I'm also making a lot of noise.

Pixie flaps her wings again to let me know what she thinks of me.

Just then London strides up, wanting to know what the commotion is. "Why isn't she in her cage?" she asks in a strangled voice as she spies Pixie.

"London . . ." I begin.

London is frozen in her tracks. She watches as Pixie gets more and more restless. Her wings are like a tiny, super-fast fan, and she cackles "pretty bird" over and over until I feel like clapping my hands over my ears.

"Make it stop . . ." London whispers, grabbing my arm tightly.

Olivia moves away a little, but the kids crowding around us don't give us room. "It's not a big deal, London," Olivia says. "Pixie's perfectly calm. You should calm down too."

This unfreezes London. "Pixie is not calm!" she practically shouts. "She's ready to fly away because *someone* took her out of her cage."

"Well, your screaming isn't helping!" Olivia responds, equally loud.

That does it. Pixie launches in the air like a feather-covered missile and circles above our heads. She's so close I feel the brush of air from her wings. The kids jump and clap like it's the best show ever. But London is distraught. She catches her head in her hands and ducks. "Help!" she moans.

I quickly put my arms around her. "It's okay, London," I whisper. "I'm here."

"Get that bird away from me," she whispers back.

She's trembling, and her hands are holding on tight to her head. My heart breaks at her fear. "I will, I promise." I turn to Olivia. "You better fix this, lady!"

Olivia face is pale. "I'm so sorry, I didn't mean . . ." She looks up. "Wait, where's Pixie?"

I let London go, and we all look up too.

There's nothing over our heads. No wings flapping like a fan. No cackling sounds.

Pixie has disappeared.

CHAPTER 18

The kids drift away, disappointed. London, Olivia, and I are left alone in a little circle. "Jake can't find out," Olivia says. "He'll lose his mind."

I gulp. We've lost animals before, but never something that can fly. The sky is so big and empty above us. "She can't have gone far," I say, trying to sound convincing. "She's so tiny. It's not like she can fly long distances."

"What if she lands on the ground and someone tramples on her?" Olivia asks weakly, her face all scrunched up. I can tell she's feeling guilty.

London shakes her head. "Why did you let her out of the cage, Olivia?"

I hold my breath, knowing this will be the start of another terrible fight. But Olivia's eyes tear up. "I don't know," she whispers. "I thought it would be fine. Jake makes it look so easy."

"And you made me feel silly for being scared again."

Olivia doesn't reply. The tears come faster and drop down her cheeks. "I'm a horrible person," she whispers, hiding her face in her hands.

London sighs. "No, you're not."

"Yes, I am!"

Okay, I'm officially out of patience with these two. "Look, this is no time for drama," I tell them. "We need to find that bird before it disappears forever."

"How?" comes Olivia's muffled response.

I look around. The parking lot is getting busier as more and more people arrive. Angie is greeting folks, smiling and offering them food samples. We can't ask her to help, she's too busy. Mama and Dada Jee are already tired of us losing animals at every opportunity. I don't want to tell them we can't even take care of a bird in a cage. That would really convince them I'm not responsible enough for a pet of my own.

They might even force us to shut down Must Love Pets. OMG!

That's so not happening, right?

Right.

"Standing here crying isn't going to help." I grab London and Olivia and drag them to the edge of the parking lot. "Let's start looking."

They come with me easily, which means they want to help. Maybe they'll set aside their fight for Pixie's sake.

Okay, at least Olivia will. I'm not sure London cares about Pixie even 1 percent.

But what she does care about is Must Love Pets,

and her reputation as a good businesswoman. There's no way she's going to let a client come to harm.

"Where are we going?" Olivia asks, drying her tears with her other hand.

"Let's walk around," I reply. "Look under the tables and around people."

Turns out we don't really need to search too much. As soon as we get close to my empty table where I've left Amir with Doc, I hear familiar cackling. "Who's a pretty bird?"

My shoulders slump with relief. "She's here!" I cry and lunge forward. I can see the blue-green round shape at the edge of the table, near Doc's carrier. Amir is leaning forward, petting her carefully.

When he hears me yelling, Amir looks up quickly and yells back, "Look what I found, Imaan!"

Pixie trembles in alarm and flaps her wings. "Hush, little baby!"

I'm running at full speed toward them. "Imaan, slowly!" Olivia calls out, but it's already too late. Pixie flaps her wings and launches herself into the air.

We watch as she circles above us, then heads toward the stage. Oh no! Jake!

Dread builds in my throat as London, Olivia, and I follow her. "Stay with Doc!" I shout at Amir as I run.

"But I want Pixie!" he whines.

I turn my head and give him the most evil-looking glare possible. "Stay!"

He nods and goes back to Doc's carrier. The three of us rush to Jake and Adam.

"Hey, what's going on?" Jake looks up as Pixie flies over his head. "What on earth . . . ?"

"We're sorry, she got loose . . ." Olivia says breathlessly.

"That's not totally true," London says. "You took her out."

"Oh, are you saying it's my fault?"

"Absolutely!"

Jake pushes aside his keyboard and gets really close to the three of us. "Stop arguing!" he pleads. "We need to get her back. Now!"

I look up. Pixie is a blur, but she's still visible. "Jake, can't you call her to you?"

"Yay-yay!" Adam takes that moment to strum loudly on his guitar. We all give him dirty looks. "Sorry!" he whispers, putting the guitar down.

We look back up, but Pixie is already gone again. I scan the area. There's a glimpse of blue green in the tree behind us. "There!" I point.

Jake rushes over to the tree and tries to climb it. It's long and thin, and there are no branches to hold on to. "Come here, Pixie, it's me!" he calls out.

"Hush, little baby!" Pixie calls back, before climbing even higher in the tree.

"We need a ladder," Jake says.

"A ladder won't be tall enough," London replies.

I look around desperately to find a solution. A pole? A lasso? My eyes snag on the fire truck across the street, next to the goats. "The fire truck!" I gasp.

Olivia nods her head quickly. "Yes! They bring cats down from trees all the time."

"Pixie's not a cat," London points out. "She'll just fly away when someone gets too close."

"Not if that someone is me," Jake says. "Get the fire truck, Imaan!"

I hurry across the street to talk to the firefighters. It takes a while to convince them I'm not joking, but one fireman comes with me to investigate. "She's right over there!" I tell him.

"Hello!" Pixie calls out from the top of the tree. She's so far away that her voice is faint, but we can still hear it.

"Hmmm," the fireman mutters, rubbing a hand over his jaw. "Worth a try, I suppose."

I give Jake a thumbs-up. He loses the scary look in his eyes, so that's good. Now it's his job to convince the fireman to let him go up the ladder too. I doubt that regular kids are allowed on fire ladders, but there's no other way to get Pixie down without scaring her away.

"I can go with you! Please?" Jake begs.

The fireman is still rubbing his jaw, thinking. "Only if you wear a harness," he finally agrees.

"Anything!"

I heave a sigh of relief because this means Pixie will be safe. Just then, a little body literally collides with me. "Imaan, get out of the way!"

It's Amir, and he's freaked out.

"What's going on?" I ask, already forgetting about Pixie and the fireman. I grab hold of Amir as he rushes past me, but he shakes me off and keeps running toward the street.

I follow him because he's my little brother and I'm supposed to keep him away from the cars on the street. "Stop, Amir!" I yell. Mama will be furious if she sees him running into danger like this.

A few people turn to look at me. Seems like I've been doing a lot of yelling today. I try to take a deep breath to calm myself. That's when I catch sight of the table where Doc is supposed to be, and my breath stops in my chest. The carrier is lying on its side, hay spilled out on the table and on the ground. The door is wide open. And there's no Doc inside.

Great. This is officially the worst day Must Love Pets has ever had.

CHAPTER 19

I reach Amir just as he gets to the edge of the street. "Amir, where are you going?" I say, panting. I grab hold of his sleeve and twist my hand around it so he can't break free.

He pulls anyway. "Let me go, Imaan! I have to bring Doc back."

Wait, what? "You know where Doc is?"

Amir points across the street. I squint. A small black-and-white thing is hopping across without a care in the world. I gasp. "Doc! How did he get out?"

"I took him out to play with him," Amir replies in a

small, teary voice. "But guess what, Imaan. Doc didn't want to play with me! I thought I was his best friend, but he didn't wanna play!"

I close my eyes for a second. Honestly, I just want to take a break from all the nuttiness going on today. "Of course, you're his friend, Amir," I finally say. "He probably just got scared. There's too much noise and people around."

"I guess," Amir sniffs. "But he shouldn't be in the street, right? He could get hurt."

"You're absolutely right." I let him loose and ruffle his hair. "When did you get so smart?"

He shrugs. "I watch everything you do with your pets."

Seriously? He's been learning from me all this time? I lean over and kiss his cheek. "I'm glad." I look back at the street. Doc is gone by now. There's a sinking feeling in my chest. "Come on, let's go find him," I say grimly.

He slides his hand in mine. "Okay."

We walk across the street. There are cars parked along the sidewalk. I look around, but Doc has totally, completely disappeared. "He's like a wizard," Amir says. "Like he spoke a spell and now he's invisible."

"What do you know about wizards?"

"I watch cartoons!"

I think of all the Bugs Bunny cartoons I've been bingeing on this week. "Oh yeah, cartoons are so realistic." I ruffle his hair again.

Just then, a movement catches my eye. "There!"

Doc is hopping behind a red car. Amir starts after him, but I hold my brother back. "Don't startle him."

We watch as Doc hops away from us and squeezes under the car. "Drat!" I say.

"What does that mean?" Amir asks, looking up at me.

"It means our job just got harder."

I try to think. On the one hand, I really need to get Doc out and back into his carrier. On the other hand, if I walk right over to the car, Doc will just hop away somewhere else. At least this way, I know where he is.

I hear shouts and the revving of an engine. Next to us, the fire truck is slowly backing out of the empty lot. "They're going to rescue Pixie," I tell Amir.

"Pixie got lost too?"

"Yup."

We wait until the truck leaves. I know there's a side street near Tasty that can be used to get into the parking lot from the opposite side. I'm glad the firefighters are going there instead of shutting down the street party. Angie would be so disappointed.

London walks toward us and waves. "Hey, Imaan! What are you doing there?" she calls. "We have to get Doc's act ready."

I wave back but with less enthusiasm. "I know. That's what I'm trying to do."

She frowns, then crosses the street to us. "What do you mean? What's happened?"

I don't want to say it, but I don't really have a choice. "Doc got loose."

Amir's looking at me. I'm sure he's wondering why I didn't blame him. What kind of big sister would I be if I did that? I bring him close to my side in a hug, and he rubs his head against my waist.

I hope he doesn't start crying again. I need to stop being so emotional so I can think.

London looks horrified. "Do you know where he is? Do we need a fire truck for him too?"

I smile a little. "No, the opposite, actually. We need something that can reach under there." I point to the bottom of the red car.

"Something Doc won't be scared of," London adds

thoughtfully. I can almost see her brain working.

Amir raises his arm like he's trying to answer a question in class. "Ooh, ooh, I can do it."

I turn to him, confused. "You can do what?"

"I can crawl under the car."

I take hold of his arm and pull it down. "Absolutely not!"

"Why not?" London says. "He's small enough. He can probably fit."

I can't believe what she's saying. "Are you serious? Mama will kill me. What if he gets hurt? Or stuck?"

Amir grins. "I won't. I always crawl under my bed when I want to hide from Dada Jee. It's fun."

This is true. I can hear Dada Jee calling and calling, wondering where Amir went. "You shouldn't worry him like that," I say absently.

Amir shrugs and crouches down to the base of the car. "This is easy. I can crawl here, no problem."

"Wait," London says. "Someone needs to stand at the other side to catch Doc if he tries to escape."

"He won't," Amir says cheerfully. "We're best friends. He'll be happy to see me."

I don't point out that Doc had run away from Amir just a few minutes ago. I sigh. "Okay, fine, but try not to get stuck."

Amir lies down flat on the ground on his belly and starts inching toward the car. I nod to London. "I'll stand here and help Amir. You go to the other side."

Once she's gone, I crouch down too and push Amir carefully until his little head is under the car. "Can you breathe?" I ask anxiously.

"Yes," he replies. Then he pulls his arms until both are under the car too. I hear him start to mutter, "Here, Doc, come here, bestie."

In all the worry, I have to smile. Amir is being so careful and quiet, like he knows not to scare Doc. I remember what he said earlier about watching me with our pet clients. Maybe it's true, he's learning how to calm down with animals because of me.

My mind is officially blown.

It's weird to know your little brother looks up to you. Amir's always been so different from me. I never thought he wanted to learn anything from me, or be like me in any way. "Amir," I begin. "It's okay if you can't reach Doc. Just let him hop to the other side and London will catch him."

Amir is silent for so long I start to worry again. Then he raises his legs and starts to push himself out very slowly. I'm not sure what's going on. Has Doc escaped again? Did London see him hopping away?

Before I can ask, Amir's arms appear. He's cradling Doc in them like a little baby.

"OMG!" I whisper. "You're a genius, Amir!"

I take Doc gingerly. He struggles a bit, but I hug

him against my chest like Sonya showed us. London comes and helps Amir up. "You did it, buddy!" she tells him, a proud smile on her face.

Amir looks so happy, it's almost funny. His cheeks are flushed, and his hair is all mussed up from being dragged on the ground. There's a smudge of dirt on his left cheek. "I did it!" he repeats happily. "I'm awesome!"

"You really are," I say.

CHAPTER 20

We get back to the street party just in time for Doc's act. Olivia meets us at the stage area, where Jake and Adam have already set up their instruments. She's got her camera around her neck. "Where've you been?" she demands.

"I'll explain later," I say. I've put Doc back in his carrier so he can calm down a bit after his exciting morning.

London and I start setting up the obstacle course. Jake walks over with the birdcage. "You girls ready to show some bunny tricks?"

I grin when I see Pixie inside the cage, fluffing her feathers. "You got her!"

He grins back. "I did! They even let me climb up the ladder with a fireman. It was epic!"

He watches as we put Doc's things together. Amir brings out the bag of treats. "Ready?" I ask Amir.

He nods very seriously. He's been practicing, just like Doc has.

I hear whispers around me and look up. A lot of kids and even some parents have gathered around. I remember how Pixie got scared by the crowd, so I gesture with my hands. "Hey, everyone! Sit on the ground and don't make a noise, please!"

The kids quiet down. Who knew? I guess you have to make them think they're back in school. I give some stern teacher looks, and it works like a charm.

Olivia nods to Adam. He gives a low thrum of his guitar. "Ready for some animal tricks, friends?" he calls out.

The kids clap and say, "Yayyy!" but not too loudly. I reward them with a thumbs-up.

London lets Doc out of his carrier, and he's off. Over the fence. Up the ladder, down the slide, through the tunnel. Olivia takes a bunch of action shots with her camera, which I'm 100 percent sure will be gorgeous. When Doc finishes one complete course, London claps with her hands high in the air. That's a signal for the kids, I guess, because they all clap too. I worry that Doc will get scared, but he ignores them and heads back to the fence again. "I guess he wants to go again," I say in surprise.

Jake opens the birdcage and pulls Pixie out. "How about a partner this time?"

London, Olivia, and I all look at him in horror. Is he out of his mind? Does he want Pixie to fly away again? Then I notice the delicate silver chain on Pixie's leg. The other end of it is around Jake's thumb. "Don't worry," he tells me with a wink. "This is the right way to let a bird out in the open."

Olivia and I groan. "We didn't know!"

Jake lets Doc start the obstacle course again. When the rabbit is halfway done, he puts Pixie at the fence. I lean forward because I've literally never seen her do actual tricks. Spoiler alert: She's perfection. She hops and jumps and even flies over obstacles like they're nothing. All the time, she cackles to herself. "Who's a pretty bird? Pixie is!"

When Doc and Pixie both finish their act, the kids clap for the longest time. I take Doc in my arms and touch my nose to his like I've seen Sonya do. "Good job, buddy!" I whisper to him.

Later, Jake and Adam take the stage to play their songs. Their practice has definitely helped. They know all the words, and they even act the right amount of goofy, jumping and dancing around. The kids absolutely love it. They sit on the ground, singing and clapping along. Now that both Doc and Pixie are back in their carrier/

cage, the kids can be as loud as they like.

And guess what. They're being super loud. Amir is right in the middle, being the loudest.

London, Olivia, and I watch from the back of the parking lot, arm in arm like a human chain. "That went well," Olivia says.

"We worked together, that's why," London replies.

I'm happy to see that their anger has disappeared. Still, I nudge Olivia and say, "You two okay with each other?"

Olivia nods, hanging her head. "I'm sorry again, London."

"I accept your apology," London replies with a smile.

Olivia brightens. "I gotta get back to my table," she says. "Lots of people wanted to get their picture taken by little old me."

"You mean the famous photographer?" I tease.

She blushes but doesn't deny it. That's definitely progress!

We see Angie waving to us from the Tasty awning. "I'll see what she wants," London says, and walks away too.

I don't mind standing alone. It's sort of nice after the hectic morning. I look at the scene around me, my breath catching in my throat. The whole neighborhood has shown up to the street party. Everyone is smiling. Everyone looks happy.

"You should be proud of yourself, *jaan*!"

It's Mama. I give her a tight hug. "Thanks, Mama. It was fun planning the whole thing."

She's quiet for a minute. "You were a little stressed out earlier, though. Want to tell me what's wrong?"

I take a huge breath. The broken glass in her closet has been eating at my conscience like a rabbit chewing at wires. I tell her what happened, the words spilling out of me in a hurry. "I'm sorry, I didn't mean to sneak into your room," I end miserably.

She reaches over and puts her arms around me tightly. "I understand why you did it," she says.

I blink. "You do?"

"Yes, of course. You miss your baba. I get it."

We stand like that for a little while. I know I'm supposed to be too old for hugs and kisses from my mom, but I don't care. This is so nice. It's like all the worry and sadness in my heart is less because of Mama's arms. "I miss him too," she whispers in my ear.

"Maybe we can look at the album together one day?" I whisper back. I'm almost sure she'll say no, but I'm going to take a chance anyway.

"I'd love that," she replies.

I lean back to make sure I heard correctly. Before I can say anything, Mama points to the stage area, where Angie is standing on top of a crate with a microphone. "Thank you, neighbors, for joining us today! I hope you had fun. I'd like to thank London Harrison, Olivia Gordon, and

Imaan Bashir for their hard work in planning this event. I couldn't have done it without them!"

Everyone claps and cheers. Angie beckons to us, and we make our way to the stage to take a bow.

Then Angie takes out a paper from her pocket. "As you know, we had a little friendly competition going on between two smoothie flavors. Well, the public has spoken, and the winner is . . ."

I squeal because I'd totally forgotten about the smoothies. Olivia crosses her fingers. "Come on, Berry Berry Wild!"

I scoff. "Ugh, it won't even be close."

". . . it's a tie! Both Berry Berry Wild and Strawberry Kiwi won an equal number of votes."

"Hooray!" Olivia and I screech and hug each other. "We both won!"

"You know what else we won?" London asks cheekily. "Free smoothies for life!"

MUST LOVE PETS

Turn the page for a special sneak peek of

Dog's Best Friend!

It's decided. Candy will come to my house as an official pet-sitting client.

Uncle Tommy agrees to the plan almost instantly, which surprises me. He asks zero questions, just says, "Send me the bill in a text message," then rushes out of London's house like Boots is after him.

Since it's Boots we're talking about, the possibility definitely exists. She's got a nasty habit of lying in wait for her enemies and sneaking up on them when they least expect it. Once, she jumped on my shoelaces and tore them to shreds.

I try not to wear sneakers to London's house anymore.

We lug Candy's carrier up the street to my house. Or at least, London and I lug it. Olivia follows behind, chattering all the way. "Isn't it weird how your uncle rushed away, London?" she asks.

"He had a plane to catch," she replies.

"Isn't it also weird that he didn't want to know anything about our company?" Olivia continues. "Most clients have tons of questions. How much it will cost. How we'll take care of the pet. How much experience we have."

"So many questions!" I agree.

"He trusts me," London says. "He was already planning to leave Candy with me."

"Still," Olivia says. "Isn't it weird he didn't leave us with a bag or anything for Candy? Like, where are her toys? Her dog bed? Her treats?"

Hmm, that *is* weird. Uncle Tommy had handed

over a plastic bag with two cans of dog food. Nothing else. I stop walking and give London a sideways glance. "Maybe he forgot," I suggest.

London doesn't seem concerned. She keeps walking, pulling me with her. "Boots probably scared his good sense away," she says.

"Should we call him?" I ask.

"No need," London replies in her usual airy tone. "We can figure it out."

"Yes, but isn't it weird . . ." Olivia starts again.

"Shush, girl!" London snaps.

"But I'm just saying . . ."

Thankfully, we reach my house before my two besties have a fight over a dog we haven't even seen yet. If you ask me, that's the weirdest part of this entire situation. We've never taken on a new pet without a single idea of what she looks like.